The Author Meets the Outlaw

The stranger smiled.

"You're Mark Twain, aren't you?" he asked as he offered his hand. "Then we know each other. Oh, we've never met—but we know each other. I reckon you and I are the best in our lines."

With this, he swept back the still-unbuttoned frock coat with his free hand just enough to plainly reveal the butt of a revolver.

"It's all right," he said. "I ain't going to hurt you none."

I clasped his hand, remarking to myself on its small size and slender fingers. As we shook, he held his cane in the crook of his left arm and placed his left hand over mine. The very tip of the middle finger of that hand was missing.

After shaking, I returned my hands to my pockets.

I could only guess as to what throne of greatness the stranger held, and I was reluctant to do even that. I gazed out upon the June afternoon, toward the drowsy sky, then up at the shuttered building, all to avoid asking the painfully obvious. The stranger waited patiently. I should have taken my leave, but damned curiosity won out.

"What's your name?" I asked.

The stranger smiled.

"Jesse James," he drawled.

Also by Max McCoy

HOME TO TEXAS

THE SIXTH RIDER

SONS OF FIRE

THE WILD RIDER

*Books in the Indiana Jones
series by Max McCoy*

INDIANA JONES AND THE
DINOSAUR EGGS

INDIANA JONES AND THE
HOLLOW EARTH

INDIANA JONES AND THE
PHILOSOPHER'S STONE

INDIANA JONES AND THE
SECRET OF THE SPHINX

MAX McCOY

JESSE

A Novel of the
Outlaw Jesse James

BANTAM 🙶 BOOKS
New York Toronto London
Sydney Auckland

JESSE
A Novel of the Outlaw Jesse James
A Bantam Book/July 1999

ISBN 0-553-57178-8

Published simultaneously in the United States and Canada

Bantam Books are published by Bantam Books, a division of Random House, Inc. Its trademark, consisting of the words "Bantam Books" and the portrayal of a rooster, is Registered in U.S. Patent and Trademark Office and in other countries. Marca Registrada. Bantam Books, 1540 Broadway, New York, New York 10036.

PRINTED IN THE UNITED STATES OF AMERICA

OPM   10   9   8   7   6   5   4   3   2   1

Between eight and nine o'clock this morning, Jesse James, the Missouri outlaw, before whom the deeds of Fra Diavolo, Dick Turpin and Schinderhannes dwindled into insignificance, was instantly killed by a boy twenty years old, named Robert Ford, at his temporary residence, on the corner of Thirteenth and Lafayette streets, in this city.

—THE ST. JOSEPH EVENING NEWS,
April 3, 1882

What's the use of you learning to do right, when it's troublesome to do right and ain't no trouble to do wrong, and wages is just the same?

—HUCKLEBERRY FINN

Reports of my death are greatly exaggerated.

—MARK TWAIN,
*on newspaper reports that he had died while
on tour in the Sandwich Islands*

JESSE

A Word of Explanation

THE CURIOUS MANUSCRIPT you now hold began as something of a literary detective story while I was a graduate student in Dr. Gary Bleeker's class on Mark Twain at Emporia (Kansas) State University in the fall of 1993. In those far-off days, when I still harbored an ambition to become a university professor and have folks address me as "doctor," I was eager to impress my betters with scholarship and hard work. Frankly, I was lazy and my work was lacking. But as with most human endeavors, luck proved more than a substitute for hard work.

My particular luck came in the form of Gene DeGruson, a special-collections librarian and historian. When I mentioned that I was searching for primary material on Mark Twain, his eyes seemed to focus on some distant point beyond the walls of the coffee shop and he said in his characteristically gentle voice that he might have something of interest. But, he warned, the material was incomplete, and came not from Twain, but his literary executor, Albert Bigelow Paine. Mixed in with the papers—which consisted mostly of legal documents discarded from the Bourbon County, Kansas, District Court—were some jumbled typewritten sheaves, DeGruson said, that looked to be from a manuscript of sorts.

And he had found the material in a pile of trash.

Now, DeGruson had been an invaluable source of historical background since my days as a five-dollar-an-hour reporter on the local newspaper, and later when I launched my fiction-writing career with a modest novel about a young man who rides with his notorious older brothers, the Daltons.

So, when DeGruson said he might have something helpful—well, experience had taught me to pay attention. The caution that he had found the material in what was otherwise considered trash did nothing to cool my curiosity. In fact, DeGruson had rescued the original text of Upton Sinclair's *The Jungle* from a Southeast Kansas trash dump; the restored manuscript was later edited and published with a foreword by DeGruson, and the resulting contribution to scholarship (the original differed markedly in tone and force from the widely published editions of the exposé on the turn-of-the-century meatpacking industry) had earned him a brief spot on the *Today* show.

The material that inspired *this* book came from what DeGruson characterized as a junk shop in Fort Scott, Kansas. The place had once been a home but had been subsumed into the headquarters of a sprawling junk lot; rusted and irredeemable appliances littered the yard, DeGruson remembered, and the path to the door serpentined around heaps of scrap metal, slag glass, and hubcaps. Inside the house it was much worse. It was difficult to walk without stumbling, and DeGruson wondered how the proprietress—a white-haired old woman in a Wal-Mart print dress and a perpetual smoker of Lucky Strikes—managed without breaking bones. When he inquired if any historical papers were about, she jerked a thumb over her shoulder toward what had once been the parlor.

Heaped around a cold and ancient potbellied stove were mounds of yellowing and mildewed papers. DeGruson discovered that the bulk of material consisted of originals from the Bourbon County District Court, and the cases ranged from thirty to more than one hundred years old.

Gene was not surprised to find the papers. Important historical documents are discarded with frightful regularity by unwitting custodians who judge them of no significance. After pawing through a few stacks, the name of a defendant on some nineteenth-century court papers caught Gene's eye: Albert Bigelow Paine.

Now, Gene did not remember immediately who Paine was other than a dim recollection that he had written some children's books. But he scooped these papers up, along with others that looked promising at the time, and hauled them back to his office in Special Collections on the library's fourth floor at Pittsburg (Kansas) State University. When he had time to investigate the name, he discovered that not only was Albert Bigelow Paine a sometimes writer of children's books, he was also Twain's official biographer and the literary executor of his estate. In fact, many sources agreed, Paine was the single most powerful influence on the author in the last decade of his life.

Although Paine is ubiquitous in Twain biographies, the biographers seemed to know little of his background other than that he came from Kansas and insinuated himself into Twain's household after meeting the great author in 1901. When his past was mentioned at all, the references were vague; Paine had been a photographer for a time, some said, and had dabbled in poetry. Encouraged by a sale to *Harper's Weekly*, he moved to New York in 1895.

At least, that's the official version.

The real reason for the move—perhaps *flight* would be

more descriptive—was revealed in the papers that Gene
had stumbled across in the junk shop: Paine was a bigamist.
From 1892 to 1895 he apparently maintained separate
families in Fort Scott and nearby Lamar, Missouri.

The papers that DeGruson found were, unfortunately, incomplete; the conclusion of the court case (and
whether the first Mrs. Paine received any satisfaction,
much less justice) are matters of conjecture. Perhaps the
rest of this literary apocrypha will be found one day in another pile of supposed trash. But the first part of the story
they relate is unambiguous—Albert Bigelow Paine, the
beloved children's author and confidant of Mark Twain,
was married to two women at the same time. Supporting
documentation (in the form of newspaper clippings of
both marriages, city directories, and other marginalia left
by late nineteenth-century living) leaves us with little
doubt that Paine, for many years, carried on a secret life.

As to the manuscript itself, it is largely complete. It
purports to be an autobiographical account of the life of
the outlaw Jesse James, as told to Mark Twain.

DeGruson found it among the court papers and
managed to assemble the pages in seeming order. Unfortunately, like the manuscript of *The Mysterious Stranger*,
it is in typescript and none of it is holographic—that is to
say, it was pounded out on an early typewriter and not in
longhand. Handwriting analysis would have gone far to
establish its authenticity, or lack thereof. Also, no ex-
planatory notes were found with it, and no overt claim to
authorship was made.

Worse, the manuscript is obviously incomplete.

Most of the two hundred sixty-seven surviving pages
were, at some point in the distant past, damaged by fire. Although many show only minor damage—charring around
the edges, for example— some key passages were rendered

illegible, and a few of the pages were reduced to jigsaw puzzle-like fragments. Was the manuscript tossed into a stove by an author disgusted by his own work, only to be rescued a few minutes later by unknown hands?

As strange as it may seem, Twain claimed that he had indeed met Jesse James, although under different circumstances than those presented in the manuscript. As recounted in a few short paragraphs by Opie Read in *Mark Twain and I*, the pair met briefly in Missouri. But the story may be nothing more than a vehicle for a self-aggrandizing Twain anecdote: the outlaw, Twain said, introduced himself with the comment, "Guess you and I are 'bout the greatest in our line."

No other clues can be found that Twain had the slightest interest in the outlaw, who was both the most loved and the most hated man for a generation of Americans. Some of the themes involved in the story, however, seem close to Twain's heart—particularly the device of swapped identities, which suggests that Jesse James may not have died on April 3, 1882.

Many were unwilling to believe that Jesse was killed by "the dirty little coward" Robert Ford at St. Joseph, Missouri, on that long-ago morning, and more than a few have stepped forward claiming to be the famous outlaw in old age—although experts have denounced them as charlatans all.

The matter was apparently laid to rest once and for all in the summer of 1995, when a top forensics team led by Professor James Starrs exhumed Jesse's grave at Mt. Olivet Cemetery at Kearney, Missouri, and subjected the remains found there to rigorous scientific testing. Although the meager skeletal remains were determined to be consistent with a man of about Jesse's age and stature, the crowning piece of evidence came in the form of

DNA testing, a tool unavailable until the last decade of the twentieth century. The mitochondrial DNA extracted from a tooth in Jesse's grave matched the DNA in blood given by known James descendants, and the debate was declared over.

Jesse had died one hundred thirteen years before.

And yet . . .

For the careful reader, the scenario presented in this curious found manuscript suggests an alternative, and perhaps the only alternative that would confound the results of twentieth-century science. To keep from revealing too much of the story here, and spoiling it for those who might be reading simply for pleasure, a fuller explanation is saved for the Afterword.

Like all good mysteries, this one leaves us wanting more.

Is this a Twain piece, or wholly a Paine fabrication, or as some scholars suspect of *The Mysterious Stranger*, did Paine piece it together from a pastiche of Twain writings? Also, why was it found with the court papers? Did it somehow have a bearing (financial, one would suspect) on the court case?

Sadly, the man most able to answer these questions—DeGruson—is gone. On June 18, 1997, Gene was stricken with a brain aneurysm and died. For several years previously, he had battled leukemia. Although he tried as best he could to gather and annotate his research during the last few years, the chemotherapy treatment meant to save his life left his most valuable asset—his memory—subject to lapses and inconsistencies.

Ultimately, it is left to the reader to judge.

Editing of this near-century-old manuscript has been limited to spelling and correcting some of the most egregious errors in grammar and usage; it has also been necessary to introduce the occasional footnote, in the interest of clarity, and to piece together fragments that seemed out of place or incomplete. Otherwise, the manuscript is presented as found.

Max McCoy
Missouri, 1998

1

The Curious Stranger

IT WAS DURING my last trip to Missouri[1] that I met the curious stranger whose story I shall presently relate. At sixty-seven, I was nervously approaching the biblical allotment of threescore and ten; and, characteristic to my race, I felt some foolish desire to return to the place I first think of when the word "home" is mentioned. Also, I had become increasingly disappointed in the world and the flesh during these last few revolutions of the earth around the sun. I had fallen into a near-permanent state of melancholy, and my diaspora was so severe that on most days I would not have given two red cents to save the whole of the damned human race. But most of all I was disgusted with myself, tired of being a white-headed old fool, yearning for the days of innocence and youth, and increasingly convinced that I had wasted the best part of my professional life (at the urging of my wife and daughters) in trying to escape from this sun-drenched hamlet by the terrible Mississippi and adopt instead a more refined set of literary clothes, ones carrying the pedigree of sainted France and the days of Arthur.

Ungrateful, you say? Perhaps.

---

[1]1902

But I expect none of this to be set into type during my, or any other, lifetime. It is, instead, done privately for an old man's indulgence. Often I have pondered what it would be like to honestly set forth the spectrum of emotions of a living soul—not just rose-colored Sunday-school affections that are held up for youth, or the jaundiced affectations of romance, or the emerald hues of greed and jealousy—but the darker and unspoken colors that I know must stir in every human breast. They have stirred in mine, at least, since earliest recollection.

And they burn in me still.

When I was a child I was prone to sleepwalking and given to strange impulses that have no name. When the black measles swept our community and sent many of my age to the grave, it was my dearest ambition to fall victim and have my family attend me as a cherished but dying member; death, it seemed clear, was a small price to pay for such comfort. When the disease overlooked me, one night I sought the company of a stricken schoolmate and crawled in bed with the infection. Happily, I became sick in no time. I survived, but my schoolmate did not. Years later, I asked my elderly mother whether she was indeed afraid that I would die. Her reply, often incorrectly attributed as a jest in the telling, was I was such a strange child she feared I would not.

Other, more complicated desires for comfort burn in me now.

My fascination with death deepened during my teenage years. While my comrades and I enjoyed the usual sunshine pursuits of lying, smoking, skipping school, and running the banks and islands of the river in our own gang of would-be pirates, we were also educated in the casual ways of love and death on the streets of Hannibal. Once, I saw a whore stab a fellow to death on the street outside a Hannibal brothel; another time, the body of a runaway nigger we had known washed up on Sny Island, not far from where we were fishing, and it was indeed a frightful thing to witness what the turtles and fish had done to what had once been a human being so desirous of life. After my father died, at age forty-eight, I saw through a keyhole as the local doctor conducted the autopsy and eviscerated the old man with the same ease a butcher would gut a hog.

This flirtation with death reached the point where, several times while swimming in the great river, I purposefully gulped great mouthfuls of muddy water in an attempt to drown; always, however, my body fought back and would not allow me to conclude the experiment. And there was the public scandal of the murder trial of John Wise over at the county seat of Palmyra. Wise had pistol-whipped and stabbed his friend, Thomas Hart, because Hart was having an affair with his wife. At the trial, an ass of a prosecuting attorney by the name of Richard Blenner-hassett directed that the explicit love letters between Hart and Mrs. Wise be read to the court, and these—having become a matter of public record—were reproduced in newspapers across Missouri and in neighboring states. What public good could come from such intimate revelations, I reasoned, and what agonies must poor Mrs. Wise have endured? Since then, I have christened such inappropriate acts as *blennerhassetts*.[2]

Every community along the river had such scandals, but the details of most did not reach the newspapers, even when the affairs erupted in violence. To be honest, my own distress over publication of such intimate matters probably had more to do with my own unsettled curiosity than with any desire to protect innocents from the wilder aspects of community life; in fact, my private tastes

---

[2]Such a word is badly needed today.

sought out those subterranean places where the darkest mysteries of the human heart were suspended. Love and death are intimately and inseparably mixed, I learned. It is a connection that I have not been able to shake in nearly seven decades of living, and although I am now long past the age when I should have need of such notions, they come to me in dreams, unbidden, and leave me to wonder whether dreaming or waking is the more truthful reality.

The fictional cave where Tom Sawyer and Becky Thatcher were lost, and where Injun Joe met his pitiful end, is based on a real cave I knew in my boyhood.

McDowell's Cave[3] was not unlike other, now more famous caverns in Missouri, and from its discovery was an invitation to the bold and a trap for the careless. It was deep, mysterious, and with labyrinthine passages that have never been fully explored. It is located along the river, within an easy walk of Hannibal, and it was the preferred place for meetings and initiations of our secret society of boys. Beyond that, however, it had one thing that other caves did not: Suspended from the ceiling of one of its largest chambers, encased in a glass-lined copper cylinder filled with alcohol, was the body of a fourteen-year-old girl.

The corpse had been placed there in the 1840s by a St. Louis physician and medical school entrepreneur by the name of McDowell, who owned the cave and had used it to stockpile weapons for the war with Mexico. Later, he suspended the body of the girl in the cave as an experiment in petrifaction, which seemed to the good doctor a viable alternative—with Egyptian overtones—to

---

[3]The cave is now known as Mark Twain Cave and is an important tourist attraction in Hannibal, Missouri.

regular burial. It seems he envisioned using caverns as natural mausoleums for petrified human beings.

Some said that the corpse was the physician's daughter, who had died of pneumonia; but I doubt now whether the girl was really his daughter, because I can't imagine any parent placing his child on display in such a grotesque and sensational manner, and with the fervent hope that she would turn to stone. But grief sometimes does peculiar things to the human heart. Although the practice of preserving the dead and hanging them in caves never caught on with the funeral industry, the bizarre monument did create a sensation along the river for a spell, and steamboats made McDowell's a regular stop to allow the morbidly curious a glance at the girl who would never age.

Mostly, I would visit the crypt alone.

Although I had had some experience with the opposite sex, usually during church picnics when the irony of the encounters made them even more delicious, it consisted of little more than bussing and groping through three layers of clothing. Bare skin was only occasionally felt by roving fingers. At McDowell's Cave, however, the anatomy was on display for all to appreciate, far removed from the corruption of the living world and as cold and white as a piece of classical sculpture. Like an ancient Greek rite, the mystery was at once too powerful and too fragile to be exposed to the light of day.

By mounting a candle on the end of a stick and holding it aloft, it was possible, while dodging meteors of hot tallow, to inspect the deceased. Or, by ramming the butt of the stick into the clay floor to keep it steady, I could scramble up some nearby boulders. There, I could sit down and inspect the departed at eye level. Although she was as dead as a doornail, she looked healthy enough (owing no doubt to the warm glow of the candle flame). Her eyes were closed, and one always had the powerful impression that she had just excused herself from life for a brief nap—although the nap, at least for the time I shared her company, had been going on seven years.

Even now I could sketch the girl from memory if only I had that kind of gift. She had fine dark hair, and her face was a slender oval with a thin mouth that was slightly parted to allow a glimpse of perfect teeth that glinted in the candlelight like pearls. Her delicate lashes were closed over sleeping eyes. I could only guess the color of her eyes, but her fair skin hinted at blue. In every proportion her body was normal for a girl of thirteen or fourteen, with limbs which were well rounded but not fat. Her burgeoning breasts were made even more perfectly round by the buoyancy of the medium, and they were graced by dime-sized aureoles surrounding tiny nipples. Her stomach was flat and smooth and led languidly down to the triangle between her thighs, where a mat of silken hair adorned the natal cleft.

The only stitch of fabric she wore was a bright bow, which tamed her long hair. A butterfly bow, as we called them, in blue ribbon.

Free from mortal cares, this girl—whose name I never learned—became the unashamed ideal of adolescence. Such was the power of her beauty that she became indelibly fixed in my mind as the standard to which living creatures are held, and since that time I have nursed a fondness, at times more grandfatherly than others, for girls between the ages of thirteen and seventeen. Not for the first time, I ask myself the hue of this emotion. Where does it fit into the spectrum of my secret heart? It is purple, sometimes royal, sometimes rashlike and ugly. Can a man be indicted for the rainbow of his untried desire?

And what of that portion of my youth, so bowdlerized by my popularized account of Tom Sawyer and his companion Huck Finn, that lurks below the waterline? It is fashionable these days to comment upon the young with a shake of the head and a disdainful look, and to cluck wisely about their reckless and willful ways. Even people who should know better clutch my elbow and speak of my boyhood along the Mississippi with glowing reverence and use terms like "blissful" and "idyllic." Generally, I smile and nod and join the conspiracy, pretending that times were different and waxing nostalgic for those long-lost days along the river. What fools we are. I am tempted, just once, to state the truth for these middle-aged fools: That life along the American frontier of sixty years ago was a time of great hardship and even greater stupidity, that violence was sudden and death ever-constant, that most folks went hungry or worse, and that every Sunday the message that slavery was good and ordained by God and the Bible was beaten into us from the pulpit; that our natural interests as children in this atmosphere (when we weren't pretending to be steamboat pilots, which was a legitimate if unlikely way of escaping our drear surroundings) was play-acting robbery and murder or worse, and that whenever our authentic selves showed through, we were likely to have the daylights whaled out of us, and it is a miracle that all of us boys did not grow up to be robbers and murderers or worse.

That came a generation later, when a new crop of Missouri children grew up during the conflagration that swept away the kind of life we had known in Hannibal. When the War Between the States officially erupted, I was twenty-six years old, and on May 21, 1861, I piloted the last commercial steamboat allowed north on the Mississippi. Soon after, I returned to my hometown and joined the Marion Rangers, a ragtag bunch of would-be soldiers composed of friends and former school chums. Many of us had even played soldier together as children, but the real thing proved to be cold and damp and made me realize that I wanted no part in killing strangers who, under other circumstances, would probably be glad to *help me*. When I sprained my ankle and the Rangers moved on without me, I used the opportunity to light out with my brother Orion to the Nevada Territory and stayed out west until the war was over.

No, when I finally escaped and realized my boyhood dream of becoming a steamboat pilot, I was damned glad to be rid of Hannibal. Then, when I sought my fortune out west—and later, on the stage of the whole world—I never looked back with any notion of false sentimentality.

So it was in this dual state of depression and expectation that, nearing the end of my life, I came again to Hannibal, and suffered the admiration of a generation of townsfolk who regarded me as the "Great Author," all along feeling that some kind of fraud was being perpetrated. The town of my boyhood would have simply dismissed the appearance of Judge Clemens's boy with a shrug, their heads crowded with the numbers and schemes of everyday living. But time and distance and newsprint had transmogrified me into something different—but not human.

I have a childish suspicion that my agitated mental condition and the attention being paid to me may have contributed to attracting the stranger, such as floating quicksilvered loaves of bread tends to draw a drowning victim to the surface of the river. I was standing on the bricks in front of the house where I passed my boyhood, having my image emulsified in silver, when we spotted each other across a river of people.

I was standing with m., hands in the pockets of my linen coat, posing in the open doorway of the two-story white clapboard house that seemed much too small for the one where I served my youth, when by and by the stranger appeared. My attention had been obsessively

occupied by a youngish girl in a white dress and butterfly
bows—it is one of God's better jokes on the race of Adam
that while youngsters continue to capture our affections
far into petrification, our leathery visage stirs nothing but
disgust in them. Nevertheless, I had been speculating
rather optimistically to myself about the chances of this
creature becoming the newest addition to the Aquarium[4],
when, as I said, the stranger materialized and put an end
to my reverie.

He was a slim man, dressed in black, about ten years
younger than me—that is to say, fifty-six or so—and his
hair was still mostly dark, where mine had grown so white
as to match my suit. He carried a cane, which he relied
upon more than a little; he was bareheaded in the Satur-
day afternoon sun; he was clean-shaven and neatly coiffed;
and he kept his old-fashioned frock coat securely buttoned over what appeared to be the brass backstrap of a
percussion revolver, a Colt navy, perhaps. When he un-
buttoned the coat and reached for a kerchief to wipe his
brow, my suspicions were confirmed: It *was* a navy, and
unconverted. A ring of caps jeweled the cylinder.

The effect was something like seeing someone armed
with a broadsword on a modern London street—an anach-
ronism, in other words.

The percussion revolver was the kind of weapon that
had fallen out of favor a generation or more ago; Yankee
ingenuity had devised newer and better ways of killing
the human animal (for a revolver falls far short at dis-
patching any game larger than the creature that invented
it). The percussion revolver had reached its grim zenith
in the hands of the guerrilla chieftain Quantrill, his mad
lieutenant, Bloody Bill Anderson, and the scores of grim-

---

[4]Twain's club of adolescent girls. Each received a pin in the shape of an
angelfish, and lavish if not unwelcome attention from the aging author.

faced men that followed them. It had been the first reliable firearm to offer six shots as fast as you could pull the trigger, but unless it was rigorously cleaned and carefully loaded and capped (by means of a ram slung under the barrel that seated the ball on the powder, and a tiny bright percussion cap placed on the nipple at the rear of each chamber), it was prone to misfire—or worse. If the business ends of the chambers weren't properly sealed with tallow, axle grease, or whatever dampening substance could be substituted, then the revolver could chain-fire. A spark from the fired chamber could jump to an adjacent and misaligned chamber, turning the entire contraption into a handheld bomb, as likely to send a spring or a bit of iron into your own skull as it was to throw lead at whomever you were aiming at.

It is not that I am fond of guns, because I am not. But I had seen enough of these guns up and down the river in my piloting days, and then during my sojourn in California, and later everywhere abroad.

And it was not simply this business of the antique gun that made the stranger differ from the scores of the idle curious that had poured out upon the dusty streets of Hannibal to see the cigar-wreathed circus that I had become. There was something about his bearing that conveyed energy and calm at once, like a well-wound spring ready to be tripped. Also, his eyes were the most chilling shade of blue, and they watched with a passionate disinterest that made my spine tingle. The stranger's gaze seemed to drive the temperature down, as if a cloud had passed before the sun. Those eyes seemed to tap directly into my soul. They were weary eyes, eyes (I fancied) that had seen the worst of the human animal, eyes that rendered me once again a small, frightened boy. For a moment I became disturbed, afraid that the stranger would step from the crowd and pronounce me to be the fraud I was.

And there was something else. As I have said, my mind had grown increasingly mired in melancholy during the last few years, caused both by a natural inclination for the morbid and by family losses that are too painful to chronicle here. The effects of age had also taken their toll on my mental state. Frankly, more than once I pondered whether a human being was little more than a bag of skin containing offal. And yet I planned the pilgrimage to Missouri in some small, bittersweet hope that those feelings of youth that had once stirred my pen could again be refined and captured. I wished to return (at least in my work) to the sun-drenched river and the days of my youth, to feel hope once again stir in my aged breast. And what was it that a young acquaintance of mine had once said? *That it is a fundamental act of hope to write a book.* I had the feeling, however, that death himself was dogging my footsteps, and when I saw the stranger in the crowd, I had no doubt.

Death had come home to greet me with an antique gun.

But the stranger kept his place until the photographers had exhausted themselves and the curious had become bored, and the subject was finally left in peace for a few moments with his thoughts and his cigar. For this last trip to the state of my birth I had left back east what remained of my family; even that ever-constant source of annoyance and amusement, Paine[5], the family dog, had been eluded. So, caught suddenly without defenses, the

---

[5]Albert Bigelow Paine met Mark Twain in 1901 and soon became his business manager and official biographer. After Twain's death in 1910, Paine became his literary executor. During Twain's last visit to Missouri, Paine was indeed left behind.

stranger found me to be an easy target. Although I turned and pretended to be occupied with some weighty mental matter, the stranger approached.

"Pardon me," he said as gently he touched my sleeve. "But I believe we know each other, sir."

"I'm sorry," I said, trying to avoid the chill of those blue eyes. "You are mistaken. We have never met."

The stranger smiled.

"You're Mark Twain, aren't you?" he asked as he offered his hand. "Then we know each other. Oh, we've never met—but we know each other. I reckon you and I are the best in our lines."

With this, he swept back the still-unbuttoned frock coat with his free hand just enough to plainly reveal the butt of the revolver.

"It's all right," he said. "I ain't going to hurt you none."

I clasped his hand, remarking to myself on its small size and slender fingers. As we shook, he held the cane in the crook of his left arm and placed his left hand over mine. The very tip of the middle finger of that hand was missing.

After shaking, I returned my hands to my pockets.

I could only guess as to what throne of greatness the stranger held, and I was reluctant to do even that. I gazed out upon the June afternoon, toward the drowsy sky, then up at the shuttered building, all to avoid asking the painfully obvious. The stranger waited patiently. I should have taken my leave, but damned curiosity won out.

"What's your name?" I asked.

The stranger smiled.

"Jesse James," he drawled.

I could not have been more surprised had the stranger told me he was the devil himself. Or perhaps I could not have been less surprised. No matter. I did my best to shake off the remark as a joke, a failed attempt at levity, or the ravings of a madman. But there was something persuasive in the stranger's demeanor, a calm determination that said more than words. Whether I believed him or not, this man truly believed he was the great outlaw whom history records was shot to death in 1882.

"I thought you were dead."

"I reckon I'm not," the stranger said.

There we were, two old fools—one in white, the other in black—chatting about the resurrection of America's most famous outlaw as casually as others might discuss the weather.

"Then, you're back," I surmised. "From the dead, I mean."

"That's what I'm here to talk to you about," the stranger said. "Peculiar that we should both come back to Missouri at the same time, isn't it? I reckoned it was a sign. They dug up my grave last week. I watched while they took a skull out of the dirt and handed it to my boy to examine. He was game enough to put his finger in the hole they say killed his old man. Except, he's not much of a boy anymore; he's a grown man with babies of his own."

"Time passes," I offered weakly.

"Strange," he said. "They were digging up my body so they could move it to a plot at a cemetery in Kearney so Zee and I could be together."

At this point, some newly curious drifted by, and forced a few minutes of small talk concerning the lectures I planned to give to the Sunday schools, the diplomas I would hand out at the high school, and generally every other damned thing planned for me during my five days in Hannibal.

Finally, the interlopers left.

"It wasn't your skull," I ventured to say.

"No," he said.

"Then, whose?"

"It doesn't matter," he said.

"I'll bet it did to the owner," I said.

The stranger laughed. It was a dry, brittle laugh, like ice breaking on the river.

"What do you want with me?" I asked uneasily.

"I told you," he said. "You're the best. I don't read much, and can't write a lick. But I have a story that needs to be told. My brother Buck could do it, but he doesn't have the temper for it. Don't you think we ought to find someplace where we can sit down and talk for a spell?"

I nodded—and with that nod I agreed to climb into bed with a new and equally fascinating infection.

2

Infernal Lies

F YOU ARE who you say you are," I said slowly while I struck a match on the rough planks of the porch beneath my right hand, "then more lies have been told about your death than that of Jesus H. Christ."

We we sitting on the screened porch of the Bixby Hotel on Maple Street, drinking sugary iced tea, seeking relief from the heat while the afternoon drowsed on. Although I was still convinced there was a good chance the stranger was the devil—or at least one of his trusted lieutenants—my curiosity had gotten the better of my fear. And, although I had stated that I remained unconvinced of his claimed identity, I allowed as to how he was welcome to follow me back to the hotel and tell me his story or not—as he wished.

I brought the sputtering match to the end of my cigar and puffed vigorously, while squinting my eyes against the conflagration in order to observe the stranger's reaction to my statement.

His blue eyes clouded and he frowned in my direction.

"Do not take the Lord's name in vain," he said without looking at me. "That's one of the original commandments."

"I've heard of them," I said. "It seems to me there are

a few others, including one about not killing. How do you reckon you stand with your Lord on that one?"

"An eye for an eye," he said.

The stranger took out a pocket knife and proceeded to pare his yellowed nails, letting the droppings fall between the well-shined toes of his black boots.

"But you are right about those lies," he said at last. "Lies about everything connected with me and my brother. And not just lies, but damned lies—outrageous lies, lies that are a slap in the face of my family's sacred honor. Why, half the books you read paint me and my brother Frank as childhood killers, drowning kittens and pulling the wings off birds and such. And that's not the worst of it."

"See here," said I, using the glowing tip of the cigar for punctuation. "I consider myself something of an authority on lies. When you mention a lie to me, you are talking serious business. Also, you underestimate the quantity of entertainment a dead cat can afford a young boy. Now, there's value."

He looked at me woodenly.

"Oh, I've never killed one personally," I explained. "But I was never fool enough to let the remains of one go to waste. During my childhood, there was no shortage of superstitious nonsense which required a dead cat as the key ingredient for conjuring the spirits of the recently murdered. Surely it was the same where you grew up."

The stranger shook his head sadly.

"Our games were somewhat different," he said.

"Tell me about your boyhood," I suggested.

"Ain't much to tell," he said, still concentrating on his nail trimming. "My brother Frank and I grew up during rough times, and we became rough men. It has been our rough ways that put us at odds with genteel society and paid us with regret."

He closed his eyes for a moment.

"I reckon that what most folks want to hear about is my career leading the James-Younger Gang, and how we stuck it to the Yankee banks and railroads, and how we eluded the Pinkertons for eighteen years—"

"And Northfield," I suggested.

"And Northfield," he allowed.

"And the truth of what happened afterward at Hanska Slough," I said. "And, of course, how you managed to survive assassination in St. Joseph in 1882."

"Yes," he said.

"But we will get to those issues, by-and-by," I said.

"I will tell the truth about the Yankees."

"No, you misunderstand me," I said impatiently. "I didn't ask for an editorial, or a defense of your actions. At least, not yet. Tell me instead about what it was like when you grew up. Give me the details, the everyday things that accumulate to make a life."

"Where should I start?"

"At the beginning," I urged.

"How much time do you have?"

"Two or three days. It is enough. Before you tell me about the man, first describe to me the child."

The pocket knife stopped. He flicked the blade shut and returned it to his vest pocket. Then he closed his eyes and leaned back in his chair. The breeze ruffled the wisps of reddish-brown hair across his forehead, and the corners of his mouth curled just slightly, as if he were savoring the feel of sunshine on his face.

"That's easy," he said. "The child begins with its mother."

3

A Pedigree

MY MOTHER WAS Zerelda Elizabeth Cole," the stranger said pleasantly. "She was born in Kentucky and her father, James Cole, was of good Pennsylvania stock but was killed in a horse accident when she was only two years of age.

"Zerelda, her mother, and her younger brother, Jesse—for whom I am named—then lived at the Black Horse Tavern on the old Frankfort-Lexington Road for nearly ten years. The tavern was an old-fashioned roadhouse owned by father-in-law Richard Cole, and it must have been an eye-popping place for a pair of young children; such was the atmosphere at the Black Horse that the townspeople often spoke of it as Sodom. My mother was an outspoken and strong-willed woman, and much of her character may be due to this early experience."

The stranger interrupted his own story to quiz me.

"Ain't you going to write this down?" he asked.

"Go on," said I, rolling my cigar between my right thumb and index finger and watching the ashes fall away from the tip. "I'm a good listener."

"I don't intend on repeating it," the stranger said.

"You won't have to," I said. "Besides, I'll make up my

own mind whether it is worth repeating. If it is, I'll remember it. Now, go on."

"All right," he said sullenly.

"Oh, wait. What kind of horse accident was it?"

"I don't know. The usual kind, I suppose—being dragged through a fence or stamped to death. Now, where was I?"

"We were getting the obligatory begetting out of the way," I said. "And it has taken almost as much time as it did the first time around."

"As I was saying," the stranger continued, "when the father-in-law, Richard Cole, died in 1837, my grandmother Sallie married a widower with six children. But my mother despised this new stepfather, and when the rest of the family moved out west, Mother stayed behind with an uncle at Stamping Ground, Kentucky."

"Why do you suppose your mother hated her stepfather?" I asked.

"Why do you keep interrupting?"

"Because you keep leaving out important information," I said. "This is important. Did she ever tell you whey she hated this man so much?"

"His name was Thomason."

"All right, at least we have a name for him now. Was it just that he was a widower with half a dozen brats competing for your mother's attention, or was it something more? Did he beat her?"

"Yes," he said.

"So the stepfather was cruel. Was he more than cruel?"

"What are you getting at?"

"How old was she when your grandmother remarried?"

"I don't know," he said. "I haven't thought about it."

"Well," I said. "She was born in—what did you say?—'twenty-five. Her father was killed in a tragic but anonymous horse accident a couple of years later, and they spent the next decade or so at a den of iniquity called the Black Horse Tavern. So she would have been twelve or thirteen."

"I suppose that is correct."

"Then we have uncovered an important detail here. For two men who have lived in the world for some decades, it shouldn't be necessary to elaborate on the importance of this detail. But your mother never said anything that might confirm this?"

"Perhaps," he said.

The stranger shifted uncomfortably in the straight-backed chair. He removed his hat, wiped his brow with his kerchief, and rested his wrists on his knees and held the hat by its brim.

"What's the matter?" I asked.

"You are asking about things that are not a proper part of the story," he complained.

"You mean, they are not an accepted part of the legend. This disappoints me in you. I thought you wanted to refute the lies."

"I do," he stammered. "But that should not require disgracing my mother's reputation. She is still alive, you know."

"Good Lord," I sputtered. "How old is she?"

"Seventy-seven," he answered.

"A remarkable achievement," I said. "Particularly considering her contribution to American history. Why, Dick Turpin's mother would have been no less proud, I'm sure."

"She is an exceptional woman," the stranger said reverently. "Now, if I agree to continue my story, will you promise to quit interrupting and not jump to conclusions?"

"Granted," said I, "but only on the condition you agree to tell the truth whole, even those things you do not consider to be important, and not parcel it up to suit yourself—and with the added qualification that if you say something even a moron of a local government attorney would recognize as a certifiable whopper, I will call you on it."

"Why should I agree?" he asked. "You already seem to be twisting things around to suit yourself. I'm afraid of what you might do with my story."

"I'll tell you how it is, stranger," I said, crossing my legs and leaning toward him. "History belongs to everybody. And whether you like it or not, you're a bona-fide part of American history; at some point along the way, whether for bad or good, something happened to transform you into our leading American folk hero—an apotheosis, if you will. Like Alexander the Great or Christ or George Washington. Tell me, do you feel like a hero?"

"No."

"Of course not. And you're in a bad spot—you're supposed to be martyred and beyond the prosecutor's reach for the hanging offenses of robbery and murder. But you know you're *really* going to die soon, and you want the truth to be told for once. Hell, the people who remembered you warmly have spun as many lies about you as those who hated you; the newspaperman in Kansas City—what's his name, Edwards?—has borrowed every story from the Robin Hood legend with which to paper your grave. So, your Christian soul is bothering you, and you have come here to confess to me."

The stranger placed the hat on his knees and brushed some imagined lint from the crown.

"Here's how it works," I said. "I don't know if I'll ever tell your story, but I'd like to hear it. And if I do sit down one morning and start to put it down, something curious will happen—each of us will get mixed up with the thing so that it will be hard to tell where you end and I begin.

Some of the words I put in your mouth you would never use given a million years—I'm not perfect and am given to more than a bit of self-indulgence—but when it's done it will be the truth . . . mostly."

For the longest time there was nothing but the sound of the wind in the trees, and insects humming, and the muffled sounds coming off the river. Oars in locks and somebody shouting to shore, although you couldn't tell what they were saying.

Finally, the stranger looked up.

"Let's get on with it," he said. "My mother met my father, Robert James, at a revival meeting. He was in his early twenties, and attending college at Georgetown, Kentucky. He was destined to become a respected Baptist preacher, the founder of three churches, and an organizer of William Jewell College. At the time, however, he was struggling to do his best to recover from the worst that life had to offer—he was orphaned at nine years of age when his parents were killed. But his older sister, Mary Mimms, herself only a teenager, took my father in to raise with her own children. Later, her brood would include my first cousin Zerelda, who was called Zee to avoid confusion with her namesake, my mother."

The stranger was so careful in describing the relationship between this girl, a first cousin, and his mother that it called attention to itself. Also, since I knew a little of the James boys' story—what Missouri native did not?—I was anticipating what was to come, and making those damnable leaps to conclusion.

"I assume we will learn more about Zee later," I ventured to say.

"You are getting ahead of the story," he said. "Now, my mother was still a sixteen-year-old student at St. Catherine's Catholic School for Girls when she met my father. But things progressed more rapidly in those olden

times, and they were married a few days after Christmas
in 1841, at her uncle's home. Shortly after, my father
took my mother to Clay County, Missouri. Then my father left my mother, who was heavy with child, with her
own mother and stepfather, John Thomason."

I resisted the urge to ask the stranger how poor
Zerelda felt about this decision.

"My father went back to Kentucky for more school-
ing, and while he attempted to return in time for Christmas and the birth of their first child, he was prevented by
the early freezing of the Missouri River. My brother
Frank was born on January 10, and the first my father saw
of him was in the spring of 1843, when steamboat traffic
was restored.

"Of course, of these events I have no direct knowledge, but they were related by my mother and other
members of the family, and I take them on faith. My personal recollection begins a few years later, at the time of
my birth."

4

I Am Born

I REMEMBER MY BIRTH.

Some folks may scoff at this, and even my brother doubts whether my memories are real or simply fancy, but I am convinced that I am in full recall of the moment of my entry into this world, and perhaps for some time before. But the memories are real enough, and they first came to me during a delirium while I lay near death from a Yankee pistol ball. Since that time, successive dreams have added more information, and on the few occasions I have spoken to my mother about these matters, she has confirmed their veracity.

It was the fifth day of September 1847. My brother Franklin—whom we called Buck—was already four years old at the time. Our farm lay three miles northeast of Centerville—a town they now call Kearney—and my mother was attended, during a long and unusually difficult labor for a second child, by a local granny woman by the name of Stutz, who employed most of the usual frontier charms. A double-bitted ax was placed beneath the bed, for example, and mother was given a potion of gunpowder and stump water. These things were meant to ease her pain, but did no good, and the gunpowder seemed to have left its mark on me instead.

My mother is a passionate woman, and although she has suffered much during her years, she has seldom suffered quietly. At twenty-two years of age, she was nigh unto six foot tall and weighed almost two hundred pounds—that is to say, she was as big as many men, and fitter than most. She chewed through a rawhide rag, kicked the foot of the bed to pieces, and threatened to whip Granny Stutz if she so much as laid another hand on her. It wasn't long before the granny woman recognized she had met her match and summoned the rest of the grown females in the neighborhood for help.

I remember the sound of that bed being kicked to splinters, along with Ma's screams and groans and the voices of the women who were trying to calm her down. I can't tell you what was being said at the time, because words didn't mean anything to me; I recognized my mother's voice and knew from the sound of it that she was in pain. It was hot and dark and uncomfortable where I was, not at all what I was used to, and Ma's heart sounded like a bass drum beating in my ears. I didn't want to leave, because things had been mighty pleasant for a long time, and if Ma was in trouble, I reckoned I'd better stay put until things blew over. But I was suddenly being forced slowly down this long, dark tube toward this patch of light. And it hurt.

The harder my mother pushed, the more frightened I became and the tighter things seemed to get in that tunnel. There wasn't room for me, my shoulders, my big head, and that umbilical cord in there. My shoulders ached and my head was sore. More than a few times, things got scrambled up so that the cord nearly choked me. By and by, things got lined out and my head squeezed out of my mother's womb, just like you'd pull on a sweater that was a couple of sizes too tight. Only, imagine that after you get it over your head, you've got to get it down over your shoulders as well. The hands of the women worked first one shoulder and then the other through, and suddenly I was in the world, when a moment ago I wasn't.

Although I was in the light, I couldn't see a thing because of this blue filmy substance over my eyes. I can't tell you exactly what I was thinking at this point, because I wasn't thinking in words—it was more feelings, and colors, and sounds. I knew my mother was there, and the granny woman and the neighborhood hens, but there were others there as well. I guess you could call them angels, because they weren't human beings and I was the only one that knew they were there. Some of them was dancing in the air, and others were just sitting high up on the furniture and watching while I was being roughly treated by the same women who had given my mother so much discomfort. They grabbed me by my heels and hung me upside down while they cut me away from my mother. Then my lungs began to burn. The granny woman stuck her rough finger in my mouth and scooped out whatever was there, and I drew my first breath— followed immediately by my first sob.

I was lonely.

They swabbed away the film from my eyes and, at long last, laid me on my mother's stomach, with my head nestled between her breasts. I was no bigger than a rabbit, weak and scared, and my heart—which was no bigger at that time than the heart of your commonplace hare— was pounding with fear and confusion. This is how we all come into the world, I reckon, as inconsequential pink rabbits, but we are made into lions by the love of those who brought us.

Zerelda was just a blur to me, of course, but I knew her—I knew the familiar rhythm of her breathing, the comforting sound of her voice. And now I knew her smell—and her touch. She felt my arms, and my legs, ending her inspection with a count of the tiny digits attached to each. I was in the safety of my mother's arms. As things calmed down a bit, I remember feeling at peace again, in harmony with the universe. I can clearly remember the overpowering love I felt for her then, and that love has continued unabated to this day.

My mother is a beautiful woman. The photographs you see of her now, the incomplete woman in widow's weeds with the sad eyes, do not convey this. But think of the best and brightest-looking girl of twenty-two or -three that you know now, and improve upon it, and you have the image of Zerelda at the time of my birth. I have always wished that I was of an artistic bent so that I could make a portrait of the seconds-old me nestled safely between her breasts, but alas! It is beyond my poor talents.

After they cleaned me up and allowed the men into the bedroom, they say my father, the Reverend Robert James, swept me up and carried me to the doorstep of the cabin to show me the world. I do not remember this. Truth to tell, I remember my father very little; he is a ghost in the long corridors of my memory, a faceless shadowy figure that I cannot conjure.

The Reverend James was twenty-eight years of age at the time of my birth. He had always seemed restless, and he pursued personal wealth as diligently as the salvation of the many flocks that were entrusted to his care. Despite having acquired 275 acres of farmland, building a respectable home, and owning sheep, cattle, oxen, horses, and seven slaves, his soul was unsatisfied. After the birth of my sister, Susan, when I was not yet three, he set out for the California gold fields. To some he said his intent was to minister to the fortune seekers there, but others suspected a more personal interest. Even a man of God is not immune to the temptation of easy riches. But there are also those who say there was another reason for his leave-taking, and that it was in the force of my mother's personality. I will admit that no man was an easy match for my mother. Outspoken and passionate, she complained loudly and often about my father's long absences due to education, revivals, and other matters that normally occupied a gentleman of my father's reputation. Quarrels were a matter of course. Some folks said my mother's affections were too strong and too freely given, but there is no evidence to support this hateful bit of gossip. A strong woman, even more so than a strong man, is bound to make enemies. And to those enemies I still say, speak the truth or still your tongue.

But what was in my father's heart when he left for California, none can say. His letters indicated that he proposed to be away at first only a year, then perhaps eighteen months, and constantly he admonished Zerelda to live a Christian life and to raise us children accordingly. He reminded her that if fate should intervene and prevent our reunion in the flesh, that we all would be reunited in Glory.

He died August 18, 1850, at a gold camp called Hangtown, of food poisoning. I never learned what his last meal was, but I should have liked to, if only to avoid it.

Being by nature a passionate woman—as well as a landed widow—my mother married again, two years later, to a bastard by the name of Benjamin Simms. Now, the main problem with Simms, apart from being cruel to our mother once the vows were said, was that he beat the living hell out of us kids. Every time he lost a fight with her, he would grab whatever was handy and start whaling the tar out of us, Susan included. But Simms was happily killed in a lucky horse accident soon after Zerelda left him, and he is deserving of no further comment here.

My mother's third husband, fortunately, was a kind and thankfully docile man by the name of Reuben Samuel.

He was a doctor who rented an office at the general store in Greenville from our uncle, Bill James. They were married the September that I turned eight, and his gentle temperament proved to be the right match for our Zerelda. I was proud to call this man stepfather. Pardon me; I am speaking of him as if he were dead. He is still alive, but because of events I shall presently relate has been little more than a pleasant idiot for the past forty years and is currently living in an asylum at St. Joseph.

Like my real father, Dr. Samuel owned slaves. We were not rich—every family of any means had one or two, usually to help with the chores of everyday living—but we were among the small percentage that, at times, owned several. A couple, Aunt Charlotte and Old Ambrose, had been with the family as long as anybody could remember. You could say we were something of a Missouri aristocracy, although it wasn't like the Far South, where the economy was built from the keel up on slave labor, but I suppose that's where the inspiration came from. It was something we hardly thought of in those days, at least not in any sinful way. Our preachers were keen on reminding us that the habit was shot through the Bible, with nary a word against it—and, as a matter of fact, the Good Book seemed positively enthusiastic about it. Later, when the New England preachers started making such a fuss, their racket seemed blasphemous. You might as well have been knocking the institution of marriage. But that's the thing with the Bible, particularly the Old Testament. I've just spoken of marriage, so let's take that as an example. It's a sacred bond between man and wife, never to be broken, two people promised forever to each other . . . unless you happen to be somebody God takes notice of, then all sorts of special circumstances apply. More than one wife is a cinch, and if your wives don't bear children, you can apply to procreate with the wives' handmaidens, and that's just the beginning of it. Look at old Lot. His own daughters got him liquored up and had their way with him, but I suppose it was all God's plan or some such, but perhaps spending their tender years in Sodom had some influence on their thinking. After all, the old man did try to trade them for the safety of the strangers that came to visit, so they might have had a different take on the whole thing, you might say. And don't get me started on poor Hagar and her son Ishmael. How do you think he felt, being Abraham's firstborn and then to be cast out into the wilderness without so much as a thank-you when their services weren't needed anymore. In all, the patriarchs were a pretty randy bunch, not to mention bloodthirsty. My sins look small indeed when compared with that bunch.

But, I'm getting ahead of myself. I'm not yet ready to confess my sins. And don't get the notion that I am in any way antireligious, or doubt the truth of the Bible. The problem is, I believe it, all of it, and just because it doesn't make sense doesn't mean it ain't perfect.

The point that I've been sneaking up on is that the world where I grew up was an Old Testament world. Sure, we paid lip service to Jesus on Sundays and all that, but in Missouri before the war we lived with themes that were outlined in no delicate way in those first chapters of the Good Book. Slavery was an everyday occurrence, and if somebody did you wrong, the attitude was "an eye for an eye" and nobody thought about turning the other cheek. Those that did were apt to get knocked upside the head twice instead of just once, and perhaps lose some teeth in the process. Blood feuds were as common as dirt. Mercy was for the weak. Forgiveness was just not in our vocabulary.

These, at least, were the lessons I took to heart. My brother Buck never saw things as clearly as I did, because his head was always full of the books that our father left behind before he ate that last meal in California. Shakespeare was his favorite; at least Beadles and the other dime libraries got that part right, because he was always spouting this or that verse and trying to pound it into the situation whether it fit or not. He got better at it as he got older, but he nearly drove us all daft before he got the hang of it.

The only time I saw my brother at a loss for words was when we had been playing Ivanhoe or some such foolishness from one of the books that Father left, when he was eleven or twelve and I was seven. We were going at it with a couple of sticks we found in the back lot. We were play-acting a desperate sword fight to the death, only we didn't know that Frank's sword had a rusty old square-headed nail in the end of it, and when he smote me a blow to my leg, that nail buried itself in the bone of my thigh. It didn't hurt at first. I remember standing there with that stick hanging from my leg and thinking how strange it was, and what an unusual sensation it produced, and Frank just stood there in a catatonic state of horror. Then he reached down and grabbed ahold of the stick and tried to wrench the nail out, but my knees buckled and I saw constellations spinning around me. I still had my sword-stick in my hand, however, and before I went under I broke it right over the crown of Frank's head.

I nearly died.

It would not be the last time that I suffered a near-mortal wound, but it was the only time that I was stricken by the hand of my brother. Frank carried me to the house and gave me to my mother, who wrenched the nail out with a pair of pliers and dressed the wound. It soon became infected, however, and the infection was deep in the bone. After three days, when it became clear that I was not going to get better on my own, my mother bundled me up and put me in the wagon and drove me to Greenville, to the general store, where Doc Samuel rented an office from our uncle. This was, of course, before he and my mother were married, and I reckon I've already given away the ending of this story. If Frank hadn't of dad-dingus near killed me with that woodlot mace, I don't think they would have gotten so close. It was an odd introduction, to be sure, but a fitting one.

My future stepfather cleaned the wound to the bone and boiled it out with carbolic acid, then packed it with grease and spiderwebs. A prayer watch was held to see whether I might live or die. It seems that I was somebody the Almighty took notice of early, because one night when the fever was at its peak, the Holy Ghost visited me in the form of a string of lights that floated through the window of the bedroom.

I was sleeping in Mother's bed, which was in a room by itself on one side of the big limestone double fireplace; the kitchen was on the other. The fire had burned down to just embers, and the room was as dark as pitch, except for those glowing balls.

There were seven of them, each about the size of an apple, and they burned with a greenish color, such as you sometimes see in fireworks, but they gave no smoke. Even though it was the dead of night, and there wasn't a light burning in the house, the room was so illuminated that you could have read a newspaper by my bedside. And although they burned with a kind of fire that did not appear to be fire, they were dreadfully hot, however, and I was concerned they would set the house ablaze.

I roused and drew my mother's attention to the lights, and I knew she saw them because she went white as a sheet and turned my head away and told me not to look. She was, naturally, terrified. Such lights are often said to hover over a dying person, and you can see them sometimes in graveyards playing about the graves of the newly buried. But I was not afraid—I was so sick that I was beyond fear—and I could not help but look.

"What is it?" I asked my mother.

"It's all right, Jesse," my mother whispered in a voice that was suddenly drowsy. "Go to sleep." And then, with the lights still blazing in the room, she slipped into a deep sleep herself, nearly falling from her chair, and leaving me to stare in wonder at the spectacle presented at the foot of the bed.

How do I know it was the Holy Ghost, you ask?

Well, I didn't, not then. But it is something I have thought about often during my life, as an enduring mystery of my childhood, and the closest things that I can compare the phenomenon to are the biblical tongues of flame that descended upon the apostles during the Pentecost. Also, an understanding that surpasses a child's understanding came to me that night. Soon after my mother went to sleep, my soul left my body and rose above the bed, to where I was looking down, and I could see my own self stretched out on that high, old-fashioned bed, with my mother in the chair next to me. I followed the balls of light as they passed up through the ceiling of the house, and above the roof, and high above our farm. I could see our cabin, with the smoke curling from the chimney, and the road that ran in front, and the little stream that snaked around out back.

Then I went higher.

The whole countryside was stretched out before me, dark and green, and I rose up through the clouds that shrouded the canopy of stars overhead.

I was as naked as the day I was born, and light as smoke. As I drifted between heaven and earth, the great river of time flowed beneath me. I saw the countryside beneath me transformed into a barren and forsaken place, where blood soaked the earth and blackened chimneys marked the spots where homes had once been.

Then the seven balls of fire swirled angrily together to form one gigantic ball, which entered my ghostly body and exploded, showering pieces of my soul over the countryside.

5

A Broken Dish

THAT NIGHT MY FEVER BROKE.
When he was sure I would live, Doc Samuel billed my mother six dollars for my recovery, and when she did not pay it he filed a suit against her in the county court. It was one of those strange behaviors that my mother often exhibited, and although it vexed the rest of us, it must have resulted in the effect that Mother anticipated—that is, it was an excuse for a continuing relationship with the gentle doctor, even if it was adversarial in nature. Marriage was just a natural extension.

I suppose the defendant found things agreeable enough, because he fulfilled the judgment of the court with patience and good humor. When my mother would storm, he would temporize, and soon calm would be restored to our little household. And even though there is a natural prejudice among men against the children of a predecessor, our stepfather always treated us James children with affection. Ever the peacemaker, Doc Samuel was a living example of tolerance and forgiveness.

Is it possible for an old man to remember what it was like to be a young boy? Strange, but I can recall the days of my youth with more clarity than the events of last week. Sometimes I wonder if memory is playing me false, if old age has robbed me of truth, but my heart tells me it is gospel.

Many will be surprised to learn that I was not my mother's favorite, because that's not the way legend goes; it is assumed that I was the darling of my mother's eye because of my charm and dash, and it is Frank who played second fiddle. But I am not the hero the newspapers and dime novels have made me out to be. That person does not exist, and if you're looking for him here, you're going to be disappointed. He is a ghost, as old as time and answering to many names, a wraith we carry around in our collective memory. Always, he comes armed. Mostly we've known him with a sword or a longbow in his hand, but times change and now he carries a six-gun. He's been my shadow for more than thirty years now.

But these are the ruminations of an old man.

I was a wild child, difficult to understand and impossible to tame, filled often with an inarticulate rage for the conventions of society. Frank, as firstborn, occupied a natural position of respect and affection. He was everything that I was not. He did well with his studies, he was responsible with his chores, and he nearly always told the truth.

In short, I hated him.

The unfairness of being cheated out of respect and affection by an accident of birth order preyed upon my mind, and I seized every opportunity to bring him grief, from attributing my own accidents to him—"Frank broke the jar, I saw him do it!"—to pelting him with rocks and clods when all else failed and I could catch him alone. Throwing things was safer than engaging him in hand-to-hand combat, because he was bigger than me and likely to beat me if only he could catch me. But I was quick and accurate, and by keeping my distance I could send a barrage of missiles his way and then be off—and at least postpone the thrashing for a spell.

When the rivalry became too intense, I would slip away to the creek behind our cabin and follow it deep into the woods between the rolling hills. There is nothing to compare to the electric thrill of wading barefoot in the clear, cold water of the creek on a sweltering July afternoon.

Old Shef was my partner in crime, although I can't tell you now exactly what kind of dog he was, except that he was large and tan, with bristling hair and the quick, intelligent eyes of a mongrel. At times I felt closer to that dog than to any member of my family, and he was so loyal to me that nobody dared to discipline me in his presence. When a hand was raised, he was by my side, back arched and teeth bared.

In the woods I felt free, and for the better part of each year I spent as much time as I could there, doing whatever I felt like. Old Shef was always interested in doing exactly the same thing. Most of the time the woods were familiar and comforting, especially in fair weather, but in bad weather and sometimes at night they became a wild and alien place. During a lightning storm, for example, it was easy to imagine the trees were inhabited by the spirits of the Indians we had driven away, or relatives of the wild animals we had slain for food.

At other times, when the sun was shining and the wind was dead still, I felt as if God were moving through the trees—and that could scare me as bad as the other. But I always returned, always exploring a little more, and I felt more at ease with my shoulders pressed against the warm earth and my eyes fixed on the clouds than I ever did with a roof over my head.

Over time I learned the rhythm of nature, of how to

stalk animals or men, of when to move and when to stay still; of how to find or keep your way; of the plants and critters to avoid, and how to make shelter and find food.

As I grew older and could borrow Pappy's squirrel rifle, I would use the excuse of bringing home some meat for the table in order to slip away. Because Frank had been designated the responsible one, I saw no reason to compete for the title, so I shirked my chores whenever possible.

Zerelda, however, was of a different mind.

My mother was quick to anger and slow to forgive, and she could nurse a grudge better than any woman alive. One of my playmates before the war was Hannah, a girl of a little more than my age—that is to say, some thirteen or fourteen—the daughter of one of our stepfather's slaves. Hannah was a house servant.[1] She was big and well developed for her age, with skin the color of coffee and cream, and her hair was rather straight and a coppery shade of red. Because of her intelligence and amiable manner, she was allowed inside to set the table before meals and to clear it after, to change the bedding and scrub the floors, and generally every other task that Mother found disagreeable or that Aunt Charlotte, who was getting on in years, needed help with.

Hannah was clearing the table after supper one day during the heat of summer, when a butter dish slipped from her hand and shattered on the hardwood floor.

Now, Mother Zerelda was heavy with her and Pappy's first child. She had been sitting uncomfortably in her chair, beating the air near her face with a fan while the

---

[1] An uglier word is used in the manuscript. It was allowed earlier because it was used in conjunction with the designation "human being."

sweat ran in rivers down her fat cheeks. When she heard
the dish strike the floor, she carefully placed the fan on
the table and skewered Hannah with her eyes.

Without getting up from her chair, Zerelda backhanded the girl so hard that it knocked her against the
sideboard. Now, Hannah was a strapping child who was
nearly as tall as my brother Frank, but she folded like so
much tissue, a trickle of blood running from her left nos-
tril. My mother had a row of dinner plates perched atop
the sideboard, and one of them toppled from the jarring.
But it fell squarely in Hannah's apron and did not break.

"Clumsy little thing," my mother clucked.

Hannah stared at the floor with eyes that smoldered
with hatred.

"She didn't mean no harm," I whimpered. "It's desperate hot, and I'm sure her hands were sweaty. Here,
look how slick mine are."

I had been sitting on the opposite side of the table
from the action, along with my sister, Susan. Buck had already taken his leave and returned to work.

"Hush up, Jesse," my mother said softly.

"It was an accident," Hannah said.

"We are responsible for our little accidents, aren't
we? You have always been a favorite of Dr. Samuel's, but I
have repeatedly cautioned him about your careless
ways."

"Yesum," Hannah said.

"We don't run a charity here," Mother continued.
"That dish cost hard money. I am inclined to let you go to
another family before you wreak any more havoc on this
house. Of course, your mother is a good worker and we
will certainly keep *her*."

A hint of fear played at the corners of Hannah's eyes.

"But, Mother," I pleaded.

Zerelda held a finger to her lips.

"You don't understand these things, Jesse," she said.

But for the first time, I did understand. I could not help but put myself in Hannah's place, and imagined the prospect of being taken from my family and sold like a head of cattle, perhaps to find myself downriver as a common field hand.

"But I'm sure Hannah understands. Don't you, child?"

Hannah looked up slowly. Her face was shining with sweat. There were tears playing about the corners of her eyes, but she did not cry. She locked eyes with my mother, then deliberately she picked the unbroken plate from her apron, held it high in her right hand, and let it drop.

I watched in horror as the plate fell. The sound of it smashing on the floor seemed to hang in the air for the longest time.

Then Hannah smiled. She touched the ball of her thumb to the blood that trickled down her mouth.

"Someday," she said, "you gwine to *lose* that hand."

My mother sat very still.

Hannah dashed from the room and out the back door, toward her mother's shack.

I rose to follow, but my mother leaned over and placed a firm hand on my arm.

"You're hurting me," I protested.

"Sit still, Jesse."

I continued to struggle.

Zerelda drew back her other hand.

I then did as I was told, and after a few moments was released.

"Susan, go fetch Aunt Charlotte and have her clean up this mess. When Dr. Samuel gets home, I'll make him deal with that little witch. I swear, she has got him in her *thrall*."

• • •

When I got clear of Mother Zerelda, I sought out Old Ambrose to ease my pain. Ambrose was not so old then— thirty, I reckon—and most every slave-owning family had somebody like him, and I suppose now we would call them family retainers. When you were sick in the body, you went to Uncle Ambrose. Not only would he cure common ailments with folk remedies a sight cheaper and faster than Pappy could, he was also the person you sought out if you were sick in spirit. And although there was a clear divide between the white adults and the slaves on the farm, that division was less distinct for us children. That was so, I reckon, because Ambrose had contributed to raising us just as much as Mother Zerelda had.

I found him out back of the shack that he and Aunt Charlotte shared, repairing a plow harness. He saw at once that I was upset. He threw down the harness and swept me up, and the feeling of his strong hands on my body made me feel safe. Even though I was eleven years old, I buried my face against his chest, trying to hide the tears.

"What is it, Jesse?" Ambrose asked. "Are you hurt?"

Whenever Ambrose and I were alone, he spoke English just as well as you or I. It was only around the white adults that he lapsed into the familiar slave dialect with its attendant mannerisms and fractured grammar, and I suppose he did this to protect himself. I knew he could read, which in itself was a serious offense, because I had caught him from time to time hunched over the bits of yellowed newspaper he begged the folks for, allegedly to stuff in the chinks of his shack.

"Come on, Jesse," he crooned. "You can tell Old Ambrose."

I tearfully related the story of Hannah breaking the dish, my mother's reaction, and Hannah's defiance.

"That is serious," Ambrose said. "But don't you worry, son. Hannah will come back. She'll be whipped, but she'll come back, and then everything will be pie again."

"But why does my mother hate her so?"

"Ah," Ambrose said, and smiled broadly. "When women are heavy with child, they become extremely jealous of other females. And Hannah is full of life and round of limb. Pappy, your stepfather, is overly fond of her. And your mother and Hannah are acting out a story as old as the Good Book."

"Which story?" I asked.

"Take your pick," he said. "But the one I reckon fits best is the one about Abraham and his wife, and the slave girl Hagar. Do you know it?"

"Go on," I said.

"Well, you know about old Abraham, and how when his wife Sarah could not conceive, she gave the hand-maiden Hagar to Abraham. Now, Hagar was dark like me, and when she conceived, it started all sorts of trouble in the household. Then, lo and behold, when Sarah did herself conceive, her jealousy was such that she could no longer tolerate Hagar or her child in the house. So she cast them out into the wilderness."

"You mean Pappy and Hannah—"

"Yes," Ambrose said.

"That's terrible," I said.

"Well, this is the way things are," he said, and he kissed the top of my head. "You wouldn't want me to lie about things, would you?"

"No."

"Besides," Ambrose said. "It isn't as bad as you might

think, because you haven't heard the rest of the story. Even though Sarah casts Hagar and her child Ishmael, into the wilderness, the Lord promises them protection and says that Ishmael will be the start of a new nation."

"Is Hannah going to have a baby?"

"No," Ambrose said. "Not yet. But she will, in time, because Dr. Samuel won't let your mother get rid of Hannah, not just yet. And when that yellow child is born—well, he's going to have his work cut out for him, isn't he?"

Hannah did come back in a few days, but she didn't come on her own—she was returned by a professional slave hunter who collected a bounty for every runaway he returned, dead or alive. Hannah looked more dead than alive. When the bounty hunter offered to administer the punishment, Mother quickly agreed, while Pappy shifted from foot to foot. Hannah was lashed to a coffee tree we had out back. The bounty hunter ripped away her blouse, unwound his heavy black bullwhip, and lashed her so severely that her back looked like something that had just been skinned.

When the whipping was done, Uncle Ambrose came to get her. Even though he told me earlier that things were ordained to work out for the best, there were tears in his eyes when he cut her down.

I couldn't imagine such treatment, and mentally I put myself in her place and wondered how I would handle it. Would I remain passive and not utter a sound, as Hannah did until she passed out, or would I fight back and risk being beaten to death? Why did my mother agree to the beating, and why didn't Pappy stop it?

When Mother Zerelda noticed I was crying too, she cuffed my ears and told me to act like a gentleman.

Like all of those who have owned slaves throughout

the ages, our family's secret fear was rebellion. Any act of defiance, no matter how small, always conjured the old memories of Nat Turner and his bloodthirsty crew hacking white folks to death down south. All of us—master and slave—were shackled by slavery, the one by force and the other by fear.

And in addition to the fear of perhaps being murdered in your beds by the very thing (well, we all knew that slaves were really people, but we couldn't admit to it publicly or else the whole fiction would just collapse) you owned, there was one other unspoken terror—that of sorcery. There was a general superstition that the slaves were in touch with some mysterious force that was inaccessible to us white folks, something that might have been brought over from Africa in the long-ago days before the ocean trade was outlawed. I don't know, but there might have been something to it.

But slavery had such a hold on our imaginations that we couldn't shake it. When all was said and done, it was the wicked pleasure of owning another *human being* that kept the damn thing running, and all the greed and perversity that naturally blackens the heart of man; that, and the fact that an entire way of life had been built on the backs of enslaved human beings.

This isn't to say that every family in the South owned slaves; far from it. We considered ourselves lucky to own just a few. But in the Deep South, the economy was driven by cotton, and cotton required slaves, and lots of them. Even before the war there were clear signs that slavery was doomed, and both my father and stepfather knew this; each had provided in their wills that their slaves would eventually be freed, upon the death of the last surviving spouse—but this probably wouldn't have inspired much hope in our slaves, had they known that Mother Zerelda would live into the twentieth century.

But it was a nice thought, and may have been more to ease our family's collective conscience than anything else. Anyway, it was pointless to argue against all the rubbish that preachers found for slavery in the Bible. The Good Book has been used to defend so many awful things throughout history, we might as well be honest and call it the bad old book.

But I didn't have any of these evil thoughts forty or fifty years ago, when these events occurred, and I never would have thought to question those things that most folks fobbed off for true. Children naturally want to believe their folks, and their teachers, and anybody else who is in a position of authority. And I remained a child for a long, long time—far past the age, in fact, when some men will come to recognize the lies that have been told. Most choose to keep silent about it, and tacitly join the conspiracy of lies; to go down the other path is a risky proposition, because it might set you free or drive you mad—and you never know which until you come dead up against it.

6

Lunatics

WAR HAD BEEN brewing for a long while on the border. While tons of ink have been wasted on "Bleeding Kansas" and the struggle over slavery in the territory—especially by the Jayhawkers, who always have had a rather skewered view of things but get to write the history books now that their side won—it was apparent to me from an early age what the real trouble was:

Kansas is a natural habitat for lunatics.

Consider old John Brown. He starts his career by hacking to death *with swords* some folks over on Pottawattamie Creek who were minding their own business and not causing him any harm at all. This is not the act of a sane man, never mind the fiasco at Harpers Ferry.

But the real problem comes along after the newspapers have telegraphed it all over the country. People naturally want to believe that madmen are being directed by a higher power, and they will go to great lengths to explain how such-and-such was directed by God to die for their pet cause. Why, the quickest way to raise an army or make a fortune is to start hearing voices and acting queer. Of course, if you want to do it right, you have to die in the end, because that proves you were sincere. Straightaway, some poet who ought to know better will scribble some lines about how good and noble you were, and what a loss to humanity your death was, and how it's just as well because you was touched by God and not meant to live on this earth anyway.

Of course, moldering John Brown wasn't the only one.

There was Jim Lane, who appoints himself the head of the Free State army, hides in a cornfield during the sack of Lawrence, and then, after the war, goes as crazy as a pet raccoon and puts a bullet through his brain.

To be honest, our side had its share of lunatics, and me and my brother rode with two of the bloodiest—Buck with Charley Quantrell[1] and me with Bill Anderson.

Quantrell,[1] the guerrilla chieftain. His name was also spelled Quantrill or Cantrell or a dozen other variations, depending on who was doing the writing, and although the Yankees insisted on calling him William, we knew him as Charley. They might as well have called him the devil himself, that's how scared they were of him. Although I've never really understood what a chieftain is, I reckoned it had something to do with red Indians, but my brother said no, that it "harked back" to the leaders of irregular troops during the Napoleonic wars. He said lots of the terms the West Pointers use are French because of that war, and a lot of tactics too; that's why back east they stood in straight lines and blazed away at each other like fools. Buck may have sometimes driven me to distraction with his quotations, but he was always top-notch at giving you the historical perspective on a thing.

Quantrell was an Ohio import who came to Kansas

---

[1]Although the real name of the Ohio-born schoolteacher-turned-murderer was William Clarke Quantrill, the guerrillas who rode with him invariably knew him under a variety of aliases, with "Charley Quantrell" being the most common.

Territory to teach school and ended up giving his lessons with a torch and a Colt's revolver. People remember him mostly for burning Lawrence to the ground in 1863. He was just a kid, really, not yet thirty when they hunted him down and killed him in Kentucky at the end of the war. He was a hero to us rebels—although kind of an irregular hero, like a factory second—and a criminal and cold-blooded killer to the folks up north. Any battle that Quantrell won was automatically called a massacre by Yankees, never mind that both sides was armed and they had promised to hang Charley and his boys if only they could capture them.

After Grant and Lee, *Quantrell* was the third most recognized name from the War Between the States—although that is sort of fading now, and I reckon in a generation or two most folks won't know him at all. That might be just as well because, as I said, he was crazy.

I reckon his family was a little touched as well, because a few years after the war his mother came down from Canal Dover in Ohio along with a newspaperman, and they dug up his body, and his dear old mother ended up selling most of poor Charley's bones. I heard that his skull was passed around for some time, and there was talk of it being put in a museum, or sold to collectors, but that it eventually wound up at a college fraternity up north, where it is used in some kind of secret initiation ceremony. It seems having Charley's noggin is the next best thing to Old Scratch himself. At any rate, he's been dead for thirty-seven years, which means other folks have been using his skull for one thing or another for ten years longer than Charley used it himself.

But the absolute madder of the pair was Bill Anderson, hands down, who came from Council Grove, near the Sante Fe Trail over in Kansas, and went stark raving mad after his sister died in a Yankee prison. I knew

Bloody Bill best, because I was with him at Centralia and after. It's hard to defend Bill, considering as how he scalped Yankees and carried their hair as trophies, and toward the last how he would ride into a fight crying and laughing and shouting Bible verses. They killed him too, and they cut off his head and put it on a spike—sort of like they used to do with monsters in the Dark Ages. But if he'd been on the winning side, I'm sure there would have been a poem or two about *him* that somehow made those things sound noble.

But I have to confess that there wasn't much noble about what was done during the war, no matter which side you was on. Killing is an ugly business. Add that to the routine miseries that come with war—sleeping hungry on the ground with twenty or thirty other fellows around you, snoring and farting and sometimes vomiting and nearly always sick from the dysentery—and you have a pretty sad picture. Then, in battle, there are the pitifully wounded, which are harder to deal with than the dead. How do you comfort a man who's had his face shot away and is holding his jaw in his hands, or the one who knows that he's going to die if he doesn't let the surgeon cut off his leg but there's no anesthetic, much less whiskey? How do you react if you love horses and the one you're riding has had its belly slit open and its guts are spilled steaming to the ground?

There is no glory in war. There is glory only in having won.

God knows that me and Buck had plenty of high-sounding verses composed about us after the war, when we began our lives of crime, but most of it was just sentimental rubbish. A regular torrent of it flowed after news got out that Jesse Woodson James was assassinated in St. Joseph. Folks had good intentions, I'm sure—particularly Major John Newman Edwards of the *Kansas City Times* newspaper, and maybe even that Billy Gashade fellow, though we never met.

Our family, like most families in western Missouri, had deep southern roots. There was never a question where our sympathies would lie, and it wasn't just because we owned slaves—although that was the powder for the New England abolitionists who aimed to see Kansas Territory come in as a free state. The feeling in our family, which was loudly and often proclaimed by Mother Zerelda, was that Missouri could take care of its own affairs and the good-for-nothing Kansans, the infernal New England Emigrant Aid Society, and all the rest of those up north could damn well keep their noses out of our business. Buck and I, nor any other member of the family, saw reason to disagree.

When the rest of the country went to war in April of 1861, after Fort Sumter was fired upon, Missouri was initially declared to be a neutral state, but that didn't hold for long—the state was torn right down the middle, with St. Louis and the east proclaiming support for the Union, while the west was heavily pro-Southern. A clash between Governor Jackson's Southern boys and John C. Fremont and Frank Blair's Union supporters left both sides bloodied, but with Jackson on the run. He issued a call for fifty thousand men to defend the state against northern aggression.

My brother Frank—who was eighteen years old—joined a home guard unit at Centerville in May of 1861, but they wouldn't take me because I was just thirteen. So I was left at home and worked for all of that summer behind a plow, fighting drought and hoppers. Then, in August, Buck had his first action at the Battle of Wilson's Creek, in the southwestern corner of the state not far from the Arkansas line. There, Union General Nathaniel Lyon pounced on the home guard of Sterling Price and

Ben McCulloch, who was leading regular troops from Arkansas, hoping to drive the rebels from the state for good. Lyon was shot dead for his trouble, and the Yankees were beaten back to Rolla. And even though the battle was his, victory was elusive for Price; he pleaded with McCulloch to launch an invasion to retake Missouri, but McCulloch refused. He said the home guard was too unruly, staffed by politicians, and resistance was too stiff. Eventually, Price dove back into Missouri alone.

Later, as he followed Price in his expedition into the heart of the state, fighting skirmishes and looking for recruits, my brother Buck was to come down with a case of the chicken pox. He was left behind in February of 1862, captured by the Yankees, and given a field parole so he could return home.

Now, the field parole was a peculiar document in the early months of the war, and it showed just how naive folks can be about such things. Basically, it offered a captured rebel the opportunity to return home as a noncombatant after swearing allegiance to the United States, promising never again to take up arms against the Union, and posting a cash bond. Of course, few took the oath seriously.

Frank sat the war out for only about a year, although during that time he was engaged in an unofficial capacity by providing comfort and information to the rebels. But by the spring of 1863, having decided that things were becoming a little too hot for him not to be actively involved, he joined Quantrell's band of guerillas permanent.

After that, things became increasingly uncomfortable around the farm as Union squads would appear and demand to know where Frank was, or what we knew about Quantrell's activities. At first Mother could usually send them packing with a barrage of well-placed words. But as things got hotter for the bluecoats, the Yankees responded by upping the ante on guerrilla activity. When they began finding five or six field paroles in the jackets of irregulars they killed, and found that much of the population in the troubled areas were hiding the guerrillas and giving them food and shelter, all hell broke loose. First came the corrupt provost marshal system, which required families suspected of Confederate sympathies to post unbearably heavy cash bonds, or to forfeit large amounts of property, most of which went directly into the pockets of the local provost.

Then there were general orders issued that guerrillas were not to be treated as prisoners of war upon capture, but were to be executed as criminals. Any family member suspected of rendering aid to a guerrilla could be arrested, including wives, mothers, sisters, and sweethearts. Many of these women were jailed in an old three-story brick building in Kansas City that had been turned into a makeshift prison.

Quantrell and the other guerrilla leaders responded in kind and unfurled the "black flag." That doesn't mean they carried any real black flag, as is sometimes shown in old pictures, but that the rules of war they were operating under had changed. The black flag is the opposite of a white flag, which is a symbol of truce or surrender. They were announcing, in effect, that since they expected to receive no quarter from their enemies, they would give none in return.

In other words, the fight was to the death.

Now, my concern for my brother was high, and I was worried about what would happen to our family. But we had fared better than most families so far; all of us were still alive, we still had our farm, and we were still convinced that the South would win (that belief would remain justified at least until the first days of July 1863, when the Mississippi fell to the Union and Lee was beaten at Gettysburg. Even so, it would take months for the consequences of those defeats to become clear).

During the time he was still at home, my brother had regaled us with stories of Wilson's Creek and other battles, but his descriptions were careful to preserve the nobility of the thing.

So, at age fifteen, I really had no firsthand experience of the events that were shaking Missouri. Much of it seemed like some kind of forbidden adult game, dangerous enough to be considered exciting but really not all that unpleasant. I was eager to be deemed old enough to play and to be relieved of the drudgery of farmwork.

All that, however, was about to change.

Oh, and there are a couple of things I forgot to mention. Things would be smoother if I had the time and the patience to lay it all out, and go from one point to another, but I don't. Remember I said that Mother Zerelda was pregnant when Hannah dropped the plate? Well, that baby was named Sallie.

Mother found herself with child again in a couple of years, and on Christmas Day of 1861 she gave Pappy a boy. It was still early enough in the war that we could celebrate the birth of a baby, because we did not know yet what was to come, and we even had a Christmas tree. It was a little tree, as was the style then, decorated with bits of brightly colored ribbon and set upon a table. Because of the season, Mother read all sorts of signs into the birth, and by New Year's she had called us all out onto the porch to look up at the morning sky, where the clouds had formed a cross in the east. Well, it was a cross if you squinted at it just right.

"Look," she gushed. "Now, that's a sign—the Almighty has a plan for this baby, all right. Just like that other baby born in difficult times so long ago in Bethlehem."

Pappy told her to hush up, because such talk bordered on the blasphemous, but you could tell Zerelda was holding tight to the thought anyway. And I have to admit that John Thomas Samuel was a pretty baby, pretty enough to make you think that God had sent just one more down to earth for some great task.

Naturally, I hated him too.

To my teenage way of thinking, the family was becoming a bit crowded.

7

Tree of Woe

THE WAR CAME to our farm on the twenty-fifth of May, 1863.

It was a Monday. When I rose that morning I had no reason to believe that the day would be different from any of the hundreds of others we had spent during wartime on the farm. By the time I would eventually sleep that night, I would know that things would never again be the same.

I was in the field west of the house that morning, working behind a team of mules, alone except for our dog, Shef, and separated from sight of home by a rolling hill. It had rained overnight. The field was damp, and as the blade turned the furrow, I was enveloped in the steaming aroma of the rich, dark soil.

The earth was heavy and I was forced to put my back into the plow and to encourage the mules. I had been working since first light, and although it was still early and the morning was cool, sweat was already stinging my eyes and soaking my shirt.

Shef watched my progress like an overseer, sometimes trotting along beside the plow and investigating whatever the blade turned up, then retreating to the edge of the field to supervise from the cool shadows of the undergrowth.

It was Shef that heard them first. He jumped up, his ears laid back against his head, and began barking his quick and shrill stranger bark.

I paused, laid the reins over the plow handle, and waited. Across the field, from the direction of the house, came a squad of soldiers. There were seven of them, in blue uniforms, their kepis pulled low, and mud sprayed into the air from the hooves of their horses. Two of them were armed with carbines, which they held in their right hands, with the butts of the short rifles tight against their thighs and the muzzles pointing up. The sun was behind them, so their faces were in shadow, and I couldn't read their expressions.

I wiped the dirt from my face with my sleeve as they neared.

"Good morning," I offered, but tried not to sound too friendly.

They said nothing.

Shef kept making a fuss, but retreated even deeper into the protection of the brush alongside the field.

Their leader had sergeant's stripes and a revolver in a flap holster at his belt. He walked his horse slowly around the mules and came up to me from the west side, where the sun illuminated his face. His rust-colored beard seemed to erupt from the color of his tunic, his face was tanned the color of leather, and his cold blue eyes narrowed as they looked at me. When he opened his mouth, I noticed that his upper front teeth were missing, and the rest were badly stained and broken.

"Where's your brother?"

I ran a thumb alongside my jaw, as I had seen older men do while pondering a question. Now, I had seen Yankees before, and had even been questioned by some of them, but there was something about this squad that made me uneasy. Still, it seemed a stupid question for them to be asking. Did they really think I would tell them where Frank was even if I knew exactly where Quantrell was that morning?

"My brother," I mused. "Now, that's a good one. Did you gentlemen ride all the way out from Liberty just to ask me that question? If you did, I'm afraid you've wasted your time."

The sergeant smiled.

"A wiseacre," he said, lisping a bit on the S because of his missing teeth. "They told me you would be. You're Jesse, ain't you?"

"Maybe I am and maybe I ain't."

"I reckon you are," he said. "Where's Doc Samuel?"

"Haven't seen him since breakfast," I said.

Pappy was working the next section over, but I wasn't going to tell them that.

The sergeant stood high in the stirrups for a moment, craning his neck and listening for the sound of work. Finally, he ordered three of his men—including one of those holding the carbines at the ready—to go search for him.

"How old are you, son?"

"Old enough, I reckon."

"Jesus, this one's just like his mother. Never a straight answer."

"I'm fifteen," I said. I was proud of my age, and proud of my size—already, at close to five foot and ten inches, I was taller than most men I knew, even if I was built kind of slight and wiry. But despite my best effort to remain calm, my breath was coming quick and ragged now. "I'll thank you to leave my mother out of this."

The men shifted uncomfortably.

"Not yet old enough to shave," the sergeant said pleasantly to the three men remaining, "and already full of venom. They're just like snakes, aren't they? The younger they are, the more poison they have in them."

"My mother is unhurt, is she not?"

"You Missouri trash think you're awfully clever, don't you?" the sergeant asked. "Lying and stealing for that devil Quantrell and his gang of murderers, feeding them when they're hungry, stitching them up when they're hurt."

"Whatever Charley Quantrell's done was deserved."

"You seem mighty proud of him. Maybe even proud enough to spy for him?"

"I'm no spy."

"And why should we believe you?"

"Because I tell the truth."

"Liars always claim to tell the truth," the sergeant said. "That's what makes them liars."

" 'The truth shall make you free,' " I said. "That's what it says in the Gospel of John, and I believe it."

"Who do you think you are to speak to us about truth?" the sergeant asked. Then he turned to the men. "This little snake is a little too big for his britches. Well, I'm here to tell you that things is about to change. We're going to learn him a lesson in manners, and then he's going to tell us what we want to know."

The sergeant took a coil of hemp rope that hung from his saddle and tossed it to the nearest of the three soldiers remaining, a big German-looking fellow with wild blond hair who caught the rope in the air.

"Of course, it doesn't have to come down to a beating," the sergeant said easily. "Not if the little rebel has any money. Do you, snake? Do you have any?"

"If I did," I said, "I wouldn't give it to you."

"If you do," the sergeant said, "we'll have it just the same."

The soldier carrying the carbine at the ready smiled as he fixed a bayonet on the end of it.

"Can't you shut that dog up?" the sergeant asked.

"Hush up, Shef," I called.

The dog continued to pitch a fit. I was hoping that his cries would attract the attention of Pappy or some of the others, but it didn't look like anybody was going to be able to save me from a beating.

The sergeant unholstered a Remington revolver from his belt, cocked it, and rested the gun on his left forearm to steady his aim.

"Git, Shef!" I screamed just as the big trooper took a run and swung the coil of rope against my back. At about the same time, the sergeant's pistol went off, and there was a yelp from Shef as he disappeared into the underbrush. The mules, spooked by the shot, dragged the plow about thirty yards away.

"Damn," the sergeant said.

I was facedown in the dirt. At first I thought the shot had only grazed me, because I couldn't feel much except numb. I struggled to my feet, spitting out clods of dirt, and was ready for the trooper by the time he had wheeled and made another run at me.

I caught the coil of rope with both hands and jerked the trooper out of his saddle. He let go of the rope as he landed in the field, then I tore out after the sergeant. I tried my best to swing that rope up into his face, but he just smiled, kept his pistol handy in his right hand, and kicked me squarely in the face with the heel of his left boot.

I saw lightning flash and went down again.

"You stupid sonuvabitch," the sergeant said. "You don't know how close you came to getting shot, just like I shot that flea-bitten dog of yours."

"Shef?" I called weakly.

The other two soldiers dismounted now, and one of

them kicked me in the ribs while the other prodded me with the tip of his bayonet. The first soldier picked up the rope and, in his humiliation, began to really whale away at me.

"Where's Quantrell?" the sergeant was asking. "Where's your brother Frank? Where did he go to meet up last time? When's the last time your folks gave them food and shelter?"

They started driving me back toward the farmhouse, and I never made more than ten or fifteen yards on my feet before they drove me back down. The going was slow, and it must have taken thirty minutes to make it nearly back home, but I was scarcely aware of it. The rough hemp rope cut into my skin like a cat-o'-nine-tails.

The first dozen or so blows were bad. In addition to the pain, which felt like being stabbed a dozen times at once, I could feel my shirt being ripped to shreds and my back becoming soaked with blood. My primary thought was that I didn't want my mother to see me in such a condition.

They kept beating me and asking their questions, and I kept silent. I wish I could report that I kept up what my brother Frank would call bravado, and told the Yankees each time to go to hell, but the truth is that after those first dozen I couldn't talk. Things began to get real hazy, and I couldn't feel much anymore, although I knew what was happening.

Then I started seeing these crazy lines in all sorts of patterns, zigzags and spirals and boxes within boxes. Even lightning bolts. It was one of the most spectacular things I had ever seen, these lines, which danced and shot across my vision like fireworks. Even when I closed my eyes, the lines were still there, and gradually I could feel myself letting go of my body. A part of me thought I was dying, and I was surprised to find out that the other parts of me thought that was okay.

Finally, I just couldn't go on no more, and collapsed in the field a hundred yards or so short of the house. I felt my bladder empty itself into the earth, and I didn't care. They couldn't beat me hard enough to make me go anymore.

And then I heard myself speaking:

"What's your name?"

The soldiers ignored me, so I asked louder.

"What's your name, Sergeant?"

The soldiers stopped. The sergeant glanced nervously at his fellows, then cracked a smile as he knelt down beside me. He grabbed me by the hair and held my head up so we could be eye-to-bloody-eye.

"When they ask who done this to you," he hissed, "tell 'em it was Danny Dawson. And I'll be glad to oblige any of them as well."

Then he let my head drop back to the soil.

Then they went through my pockets, and they cussed when they didn't find anything but a cheap case knife. They threw the knife out into the field. As they were muttering and fussing around me, trying to decide what to do next, the most peculiar thing happened. I lifted up out of my body, just like I did the night I had a fever as a boy, and I could see myself crumpled on the ground below and the soldiers standing around me, with the reins to their horses in their hands.

"I think he's dead, Sarge," I heard one of the soldiers mutter.

"Leave him," Dawson said as he mounted his horse.

"Didn't get much out of him, did we?" the big soldier said.

"Shut up," Dawson snapped.

They rode away to join the others.

I rose over the fields and drifted by the house. I could see my ma—who was a couple of months gone in the family way—and her dress was about half torn off her and she was crying. Ordinarily, this would make me mad enough to fight the devil himself, but seeing as how I was outside my body, I didn't have any emotion at all other than a vague sadness.

Moving on, I saw Shef beneath the wooden porch on the west side of the house, hiding in the shadows. His insides must have been busted up pretty good, because he was dead by sundown.

Some distance farther on, hanging from a rope that was strung over a limb of the old coffee tree on the edge of our place, was Pappy.

I could see that the Yankees had placed an eight-knotted hangman's noose around his neck and were jerking him off the ground every time he wouldn't answer one of their questions. His hands were tied behind his back and his legs kicked piteously beneath him while they let him dangle for a minute or two. Then they would let him fall to the ground like a sack of potatoes, pull him to his feet, and the routine would begin again.

The soldiers would laugh at the spectacle of this gentle old man dancing on air, and in my spirit mind I didn't know who to feel sorrier for, them or their victim.

Finally, they tired of the game, and they cut the rope that dangled from Pap's neck. They all mounted up, with the sergeant at the lead, and when they left they took Pappy with them.

When I came back into my body I lay there for a long time, not really wanting to believe what had happened to us. It must have been just a bad dream, I told myself, and if I just lay there still enough and quiet enough, it would all go away.

Of course, it didn't.

I managed to crawl down to the little creek that runs behind the house, and there in the ice-cold water I cleaned myself up a bit. Most of the injuries didn't surprise me; that was mostly because they wouldn't begin to hurt in full measure until the next day. There were broken ribs, my eyes were swelled nearly shut, and my back felt like the skin had been peeled off it. Life on a farm can be rough, and I had seen all of these wounds before, in one form or another. But the thing that truly frightened me was down by my groin, where the muscles had failed and a loop of intestine had pushed itself out. Just looking at it made me sick, and I emptied the contents of my stomach several times in the creek. It was a spell before I could work up the nerve to climb the bank and make my way back to the cabin.

8

Beyond the Pale

AFTER WE GOT Pappy back from the jail at Liberty, where they had held him for a few days after the raid on our farm, we discovered the real damage that had been done to this gentle man that we all loved: His brain had gone so long without oxygen during the repeated hangings that it had turned him into an idiot.

His speech was slurred, his mind was soft, and he couldn't do any more work than a five-year-old kid. Mother said it would have been kinder for the Yankees to have let him hang until he was dead, and I reckoned she was right.

But ours was not the only family that had been terrorized in an attempt to gain information about the guerrillas. Such incidents, and worse, were happening across Missouri, and as news spread, the boys in the bush just fought back harder.

The soldiers came back a couple of weeks later, and this time they took Mother Zerelda and five-year-old Sallie away with them. The Yankee general, Ewing, had ordered that the mothers, wives, sisters, and sweethearts of known guerrillas were to be locked up so they could not provide their men with supplies and information.

Mother and Sallie were held at St. Joseph, then were released in the first week of June, when Zerelda signed a loyalty oath. About a hundred other women refused to sign such oaths, however, and they were eventually gathered together in a makeshift prison in Kansas City.

I did my best to keep my spirits up and help Mother run the farm the rest of that summer, and although my body healed, it was my spirit that had gone soft and kind of squirmy. The wild child that I was died during the whipping by the Union soldiers, but I was not yet ready to shoulder the responsibility of adulthood. Instead, I was frozen in between, neither child nor man, with the memory of the whipping never far from my mind. Every time I thought about it, my cheeks burned, and inside I blazed with a kind of adolescent shame that could find no release.

Also, I cried.

I have never confided this to anyone before, first because I was too ashamed of myself, and later because it just didn't fit anybody's image of me. But now that I have a lifetime of perspective on the thing, I don't mind admitting it, and will tell you that it would not be the last time I shed tears for what had been done to me and my family. Of course, mostly I cried when I was alone, or in bed when I thought everyone else was asleep, and I hated myself for it—I called myself weak, and a coward, but that just made things worse. I had trouble sleeping, so I spent a lot of time staring into the dark and crying.

During this time, others began to comment on the fact that my eyes were always red and swollen. At first I thought it was just the crying, and I was mortified that folks had noticed. Later I was diagnosed with a condition called granulated eyelids, which means that my lids are chronically inflamed and crusty. The condition, which is related to dandruff, is not serious—but it is annoying and painful, and its onset was just one more indignity.

For months it was as if I had been swallowed up by a

hole in the ground where nobody could see or hear me. I missed Shef something awful, and when I couldn't stand it anymore, I would sneak out of the house and just sit beside the spot near the coffee tree where I buried him the day after the Yankees came.

A lot of people after the war called me and my brother Buck animals for the things we did, and that always seemed kind of ironic to me. I have never had an animal lie to me, steal from me, or try to humiliate or hurt me just for the sport, while I have a long list of human beings who have engaged in such activities.

Yet, I longed for revenge. I fantasized about killing the soldiers who had shamed me and my family. In my daydreams I hunted them down one by one, and they always begged pitifully for mercy, but I pulled the trigger anyway.

Also, I missed Buck something awful.

This came as somewhat of a shock, because before the war I had regarded him as a nuisance. Now, however, I found myself wishing for his company. I also envied him because he was a combatant, and not simply a victim waiting for the next round of terror. But Buck did not return to the farm after he left to join Quantrell, for fear that his presence would provoke an even worse attack.

I did think about joining him, but contrary to what has been written, I never actually presented myself to any of the guerrilla bands and then was sent home because of my age. That is just more window dressing tacked on to the legend, and I'm sure just about any of the guerrillas would have taken me on the spot—most of them, after all, were just kids themselves.

As the summer of 1863 wore down toward the fall, things began to happen kind of fast.

On August 14 the women's building in Kansas City collapsed. The women were being kept on the second floor of an old building, over a liquor store. Five of the women were killed, including Josephine Anderson, a sister to Bloody Bill, and many of the others were injured.

Immediately, rumors began to circulate that the Yankees had caused the collapse, and although that seems unlikely, it is a known historical fact that the post surgeon had advised General Ewing that the structure was unsafe and the women should be moved. Also on the day of the prison collapse, Ewing had finalized General Order Number Ten, which commanded that the families of known guerrillas were to be removed by force from their lands and to leave the state of Missouri.

In retaliation, the guerrillas crossed the line and burned Lawrence, Kansas, to the ground—and killed one hundred and fifty men and boys in the process. Quantrell led the raid and Frank was with him. Jim Lane, the notorious free stater, was at home at the time but hid in a cornfield to avoid execution.

Much has already been written of this raid—probably more than just about any other event of the war outside the major battles in the east—so I won't bother going into detail other than to say Quantrell led the raid and that Frank was with him. Buck never spoke afterward about what he saw, not even to me. Well, perhaps, but that is Buck's story to tell.

Things went all to hell after the Lawrence raid.

General Ewing issued General Order Number Eleven, which ordered the evacuation of all Confederate sympathizers within fifteen days from three counties and part of a fourth along the Kansas border. It was a little more complicated than that, as I recall, but that's the gist of it. Doc Jennison and his Jayhawkers were given the job of enforcing the order, which they did with zeal. They drove tens of thousands of people out of Missouri, and to make sure they stayed gone, they burned their homes to the ground.

Although our home was spared—Clay was not one of the counties named—there was more than enough misery to go around, with refugees flooding the countryside and never enough to eat. Although it was possible to survive during the warm months without a roof over your head, winter was nearly upon us. The roads were filled with families in rags, and often the decision to share your food meant risking starvation for yourself.

Quantrell evacuated Missouri as well.

It was his practice to take his troops to Texas during the winter, which not only was warmer, but was deep within the Confederate lines. Along the way they stopped at Baxter Springs, a small outpost in southeastern Kansas, where they ambushed a military column and killed about a hundred Yankees.

When the cold weather finally came, it put an end to the killing for a spell. Everybody was in kind of a daze, like you were in the middle of a nightmare, and you knew it was a nightmare, but you couldn't wake yourself up. It was a hard winter, and it yielded to a hard spring.

9

The Black Flag

THREE DAYS AFTER joining the guerrillas I found myself crouching behind a low ridge that overlooked the telegraph road that ran from Independence to Warrensburg. I was holding the reins of a stolen horse and in my belt was tucked an old dragoon pistol. The sun was scarcely up. I hoped the men on either side of me would not notice that I was shivering beneath the flowing guerrilla shirt that my mother had given me as a farewell gift.

The shirt was decorated with bits of ribbon and fancy stitching, and was similar to the hunting shirts that women had made their men in happier times. The shirt, and the knife at my belt, were about the only things I had left the farm with. Not even my desire for revenge still blazed in my chest; instead, it had burned down to a dull ache that was tempered by some boyhood hope of adventure.

I had no difficulty in finding the guerrillas—at least the closest group of them—because they had made camp at a farm just twenty miles from home. Everybody except the Yankees knew where they were.

The guerrillas had fought among themselves since their sojourn in Texas, and by midsummer Charley Quantrell had decided to lay low. Even though the Lawrence raid had been regarded as a victory in the eyes of most Southerners—and an unprovoked atrocity by Yankees—the regular Confederate Army was uncomfortable with it. Instead of the hero he so desperately wanted to be, Quantrell had become a pariah.

Bill Anderson was quick to take up the slack. I walked into his camp in the middle of broad daylight, and apart from some halloos and how-are-yous, I was not challenged once. It was apparent from my dress and my demeanor who I was and what my intentions were.

When I found Anderson, he was sitting in front of a stump and scraping with the edge of his knife at something that looked like a pelt. He reminded me of the pictures I had seen in pirate storybooks, handsome and wild. He had dark eyes, unruly dark hair, and a scruffy beard. On his head he wore a black slouch hat with a star pinning up the brim on one side, and around his waist were a pair of revolving pistols stuck into a belt that was cinched with a big brass buckle. I was a little afraid of him because I had heard stories that he had gone mad when his sister had died in the barracks collapse at Kansas City.

"You want to join?" he asked without looking up from his work.

"Yes," I managed to get out.

"Just who the hell are you?"

"My name is Jesse Woodson James, and my family is from Clay County by way of Kentucky," I stammered. "My brother Buck . . . Frank, that is . . . he rides with Quantrell."

"I know him," Anderson said. "He'll do to cross the river with. God damn, what is wrong with your eyes?"

"Nothing," I said. "Been sick, that's all."

"You still sick?"

"No, sir."

"Your face is mighty white. Hell, it's also as smooth as a girl's. How old are you?"

"Seventeen," I lied.

The truth is that I was still sixteen and wouldn't turn seventeen until September. But I wanted him to think I was older, if only to give me more confidence.

"Damn near a veteran," Anderson said as he held up his work to examine it. He rubbed his thumbs through the fine brown hair, blew on it to reveal the nap, then turned it over and stroked the flesh side. Dissatisfied, he went at it again with the edge of the knife.

"Thank you, sir."

"Captain."

"Captain," I said.

"That knife it?"

"Sir?"

"Do you have any other weapon than your hunting knife?"

"No, sir."

"Horse?"

"No, sir."

Anderson shook his head and cussed.

"You'll have to find your own horse," he shouted. "Steal one if you have to. I don't care. Wait. You can ride, can't you?"

I nodded.

"Well, that's something." Then he turned to one of his subordinates, a little man with a beard who was wearing the overcoat of a Union Army officer. "Bring me the box."

"Me?" the man asked.

"Yes, you, dammit," Anderson fumed.

The little man slunk off.

"If you please," I said, "I'm ready to swear in."

"What?"

"To take the Black Oath," I said. "We've all heard of it back home, Captain. The one where you swear to fight to the death and show no mercy, because mercy is for the weak. And so forth."

"Oh, that," Anderson said. "That's just something we send to the newspapers every now and then to keep the Yankees nervous."

"What about the Black Flag?" I asked. "I've seen a picture of it in the illustrateds."

"No Black Flag either," he said. "I've seen the picture too, but I'm afraid the flag exists only in the artist's imagination. It originally started out as what you would call a figure of speech, but everybody talked so much about it, they reckoned it must be real."

"Yes, sir."

"Captain."

The little subordinate returned carrying a wooden box by its rope handles. When he placed it on the ground beside the stump, it rattled.

"Look here," Anderson said, flinging open the lid of the box to reveal the sorriest collection of firearms I had ever seen. There were a couple of old single-shot pistols, some rusty cap-and-ball revolvers that had probably seen service in the Mexican war, and parts—springs, cylinders, pins—that didn't look like they fitted anything at all.

"Choose a weapon," he said.

I knelt down and probed the contents.

The best-looking candidate was a dragoon-type pistol of uncertain parentage. It had the least rust, but even so the cylinder was so worn that it rattled in the frame and the loading lever didn't want to stay put beneath the barrel.

"Load it," he said. He reached inside one of his jacket

pockets and dumped some balls and a tin of percussion caps on the stump, along with a powder flask. The balls were different sizes.

I held the dragoon in my left hand, barrel up, while I spun the cylinder and charged five of the chambers. Then I picked out an equal number of the right caliber balls from the mess on the stump, rammed them home, and capped the cylinder.

"Some grease?" I asked.

"You won't always have time for that," Anderson said.

"No, Captain," I said. "But we do now."

Anderson handed me a ball of grease rolled up in a handkerchief, and I pinched some pieces from it and sealed the ends of the chambers. I also dabbed a bit on the end of the loading lever, hoping it would help keep it up where it belonged.

"Your brother teach you to do that?" Anderson asked. I nodded.

"Fair enough," he said. "Let's hope you can use it. I know it's a real piece of shit, but you're stuck with it until you can kill somebody who's carrying something better."

"That would mean an officer, wouldn't it?"

"You're catching on," Anderson said.

He kicked the lid of the box shut and returned to his skinning work. I concluded that the pelt was not from any animal I had ever seen.

I slipped the dragoon under my belt, but not before I was sure the timing was lined up on an empty chamber. The last thing I needed was to drop it on the hammer and shoot myself before the enemy got a chance to.

"Well, is there something else?"

I had decided earlier not to ask. But now that I had gained some confidence by passing the revolver test, my curiosity got the better of me.

"Captain, if you don't mind my asking," I said. "What is that thing you're working on?"

"This?" Anderson grinned as he held it up. "Why, it's the scalp from the last man I killed. Part of my collection. I put them on the bridle of my horse, and it scares the hell out of the Yankees."

He laughed. Then he threw the ugly thing to me. I caught it, but the feel of it made me kind of weak in the knees.

"I have enough of 'em," he said. "You can have that one. Consider it your oath."

I buried the scalp the first chance I got, which was when I went to the woods under the pretense of moving my bowels that night. When I returned, the sentry told me not to stray so far next time, because I was liable to get shot walking back. When I went to sleep that night, on the straw on the floor of the barn with thirty strangers around me, and more outside, I was still feeling the ugly thing in my hand.

Late that night a couple of brothers by the name of John and Dock Rupe rode into camp, leading a cavalry mount taken after a skirmish with a forage wagon escort. The horse was a docile little dun-colored mare, and when they asked who needed a mount, I allowed that I did. They threw me the reins.

In the early morning hours of my third day with the guerrillas, we began to prepare for our ambush of the mail coach on the telegraph road. The company had swelled to about seventy-five men since I had arrived, and most of them were participating in the engagement. It was, I learned, to be the first blow in a series of hit-and-run attacks that would be based more on opportunity than strategy.

Before we rode away from the farm, Anderson led the company in a prayer service. He placed the Bible on his favorite stump and brought a lighted candle down low so he could read the verse that had been selected the day before. The selection itself, which I had witnessed, took only a moment. Anderson had closed his eyes, let the Bible fall open at random, and jammed his finger on the page.

" 'The hand of the Lord was upon me,' " Anderson read, " 'and carried me out in the spirit of the Lord, and set me down in the midst of the valley which *was* full of bones.' "

And then Anderson snapped the Bible shut without reading any more, and it left me to wondering just whose bones the valley would be full of.

"Remember," Anderson said, "if those Yankees capture you, they will kill you. They might shoot you on the spot, or they might take you back to their post to hang, but either way you're dead. Fight like your lives depend on it, because they do."

Then we rode off, and in a few hours I was crouched behind that ridge overlooking the telegraph road, holding the reins of my horse in my left hand, waiting for my baptism of fire. I was anxious and nervous and shivering, like I said, but I don't really know whether it was from fear or excitement. They both sort of got mixed up together, and it was hard to tell one from the other.

Soon the word came down the line to keep the horses quiet, and not to talk, and a minute or so after I could hear the wheels of the mail coach and the hooves of the cavalry escort as they came down the road. They were a good quarter of a mile away, but it was a still morning, and not even the birds were singing yet. But the harder I listened, the more difficult it was to hear, on account of the blood thumping in my ears. My face became flushed and my ears burned. Suddenly my mouth was so dry, I could hardly swallow.

Then Anderson, who was up at the head of the line, was already in the saddle, and he was leaning low over the neck of his horse and peering through a tangle of brush at the road. The sound of the coach was so loud now that I was afraid it would pass without us getting a chance at it. Then Anderson stood high in the saddle and waved his hat, which was the signal for a decoy group of riders to take off.

A dozen men rushed down, screaming like Comanches, while the rest of us waited and listened. Once they were sure the Yankees had gotten a good look at them, our boys acted confused, wheeled around, and raced down the road in the opposite direction. The cavalry, which believed they outnumbered their foe two to one, tore after them, leaving only a handful of men to protect the mail coach.

As soon as the bulk of the cavalry was out of sight, Anderson let out a blood-curdling scream and spurred his horse over the ridge. It wasn't a rebel yell exactly, but was more like something I've heard from a panther or other wild animal that's about to draw blood. Then he started shouting something, and, although I couldn't really be sure with all the hubbub, I thought it was Bible verses.

By the time I could draw the dragoon pistol and follow, most of the men were already over the ridge. The mail coach was stopped on the road right below us, just as perfect as if Bloody Bill had driven it himself, and we swooped down on the surprised Yankees like a pack of demons.

We did not so much attack them as engulf them. The

crackling of our revolvers was immediately answered by the boom of carbines from the handful of horse soldiers who had been left behind. The coach driver fell from his seat, still clutching the reins, while the horses reared and screamed in terror.

Behind the mail coach was a forage wagon. The teamsters bailed out at first sight of us and made for the woods, leaving the narrow road behind the mail coach blocked by the big green wagon and a team of frightened mules that couldn't decide on which way to pull.

I had fired three shots from the dragoon revolver before I realized I was just pointing it in the general direction of the enemy, and not really aiming. Besides, the loading lever had come loose and was flapping crazily beneath the barrel, which made the gun about as easy to balance as a cat in a burlap sack.

The whole affair was more difficult than I had ever imagined, and unlike any of the shooting I had done back on the farm. To hit anything from the saddle of a horse traveling at any speed requires a fair amount of skill, but when you consider that your target is also moving and *shooting back*—well, that puts things in a different light.

Also, I discovered I wasn't breathing.

I had taken a deep breath at the beginning of the charge, and had unconsciously held it throughout the first minute or so of the ambush. The intent had been to steel myself for action, but the result was that after a minute or so, my ears began to ring and my vision started to narrow.

When I finally did take a breath, it was like coming to the surface of a cold lake after diving so deep you didn't think you were going to make it up again. My peripheral vision was restored, my hearing returned, and time slowed to a crawl. Then my brain chain-fired on three thoughts at once: First there was the recognition that I was alive, and then there was the reality of being smack in the mid-

dle of more than a hundred men who were intent on murder, and then there was the third shock that at least a
fraction of those murderous individuals were attempting
to kill me.

I sucked more air into my lungs, thumbed back the
hammer on the dragoon, slapped the loading lever back
in place, and took aim at a Yankee cavalryman not twenty
yards distant who was attempting to get his carbine
turned in my direction.

I fired—and missed.

Somebody else shot him in the head.

It must have been one of our boys using a long gun
instead of a revolver, because the side of the man's head
blossomed into a froth of blood and brains. He was dead,
but it seemed like it took him a moment to realize it, because he just sort of stuck there in the saddle with an
amazed look in the eye that wasn't popped out and most
of his gray matter covering the right shoulder of his uni-
form. Then he fell. It was the first man I had ever seen
killed, and I don't mind telling you that it is not at all how
I imagined it would be.

"Oh, shit!" said I.

Then I spun my horse around, looking for another
target, and at that instant a minié ball whizzed by my ear.
It felt as big as a cannonball. By then the scene was covered in a layer of blue smoke that hugged the ground and
reduced my field of vision to perhaps ten yards. I had no
idea who had fired that shot, but I got the message that it
was unwise to stay in one spot for even a second, so I dug
my heels into the belly of my horse to get some forward
motion.

A surviving cavalryman had the same idea, except going in the opposite direction, and as he emerged from the
battle smoke, our horses collided so hard that it threw me
over the neck of mine. It was a good thing, too, because

this man had a revolver aimed at me and it popped just after I went down.

I held on to the reins and my gun, and got dragged only a few yards before I got my feet beneath me and fired a round over the top of my saddle at the Yankee. Unbelievable as it seemed to me, even at this range, I missed again.

Of course, I cussed the gun.

Then I cussed the horse, who was spooked something fierce by then and did not want to let me on his back under any circumstances. He was kicking and trying to bite while I had one foot up in the stirrup and was dragging the other.

By the time I managed to climb back into the saddle, the main group of Yankee cavalry had realized they'd been tricked, and were rushing back down the road toward us. They either were exceptionally brave or exceptionally stupid, or they simply had not reckoned our numbers correctly through the haze. They didn't get very far, as half a dozen of them were promptly shot out of the saddle. This broke the forward momentum of their assault, and we held our ground while they attempted to reorganize themselves.

I took note of the fellows nearest me, who seemed to be having none of my troubles, but who were solidly sitting their horses and calmly choosing their shots before they fired. So I circled around to face down the road, steadied my horse, then took aim with care at one of the blue figures and pulled the trigger.

The hammer fell on a spent chamber.

Somehow I had used the remaining rounds in the revolver, although I had no memory of doing so.

I looped the reins around the saddle horn while I fumbled in my shirt pockets for powder and shot, and reloaded the antique piece as quickly as I could. The load-

ing lever was particularly troublesome, and seemed to
jam inexplicably as I anxiously seated the last round. By
the time I was done, I had spilled enough powder and
balls on the ground for three reloads. When I cocked
the gun, the cylinder was reluctant to turn, and when I
forced it, there was a cracking sound.

But the fight was over, with no enemy to be seen.
Everything had gotten quiet again. No shots, no yelling,
just the crying of the horses and groans from the wounded
men on the ground.

The dead made no sound.

We had killed the whole lot of them.

Already a dozen of our boys were on the ground, strip-
ping the uniforms from the dead Yankees and searching
their pockets for valuables. The wounded were dispatched
with a pistol shot, the butt of a rifle, or a knife across the
throat. Letters and other personal effects that were worth-
less to anybody except the recently deceased owners were
tossed aside. Boots and jackets seemed particularly prized,
even more than weapons.

Somebody unhitched the horses from the team while
somebody else shot the mules in their tracks. The bodies
of the teamsters were dragged back and thrown into
the wagon—which carried nothing more valuable than
firewood—and the lot was set on fire. Fistfights broke out
among our boys for possessions.

Half a dozen guerrillas clamored over the mail coach.

"Jesus Christ, will somebody cut those damned telegraph wires?" Anderson bellowed as he dismounted.

The little subordinate, Archie, shinnied up the telegraph pole with a pair of pliers.

Anderson examined the contents of the mail coach,
which had been thrown down to the road, and took the
most promising-looking pouches before he ordered it
burned as well.

"Any gold?" Archie called down.

"No," Anderson said. "But we've greenbacks and plenty of firewood."

Archie snipped the wires, which parted with a whip-lash sound. The end of one of the wires raked the fore-head of one of the guerrillas below, knocking him to the ground. He got back to his feet a little unsteadily, dabbing at his forehead with the palm of his hand.

"Rupert, that'll teach you not to stand beneath there next time," Anderson said dryly, and the men—including the one who had been knocked down—laughed.

Then Anderson turned his gaze upon me.

I was still up on my horse, turning my attention from one group to another, just as someone who had a front-row seat would take in a three-ring circus.

"Well, nimrod," Anderson said to me. "What do you think? Do you have a taste for this kind of work?"

My mind was working, but I couldn't form any words.

"What's wrong, boy?" the captain demanded.

"He's wounded," Archie said as he jumped down from the telegraph pole.

"Is that blood yours?" Anderson asked.

I looked down. My sleeve was bright and wet with blood that was spurting from my left hand. Shocked, I clamped the hand beneath my armpit while still holding the gun in my right.

Anderson walked over and took the revolver from me.

In my frantic effort to reload, I had sheared off the tip of my left middle finger beneath the loading lever, and the bit of bone and nail had wedged between the frame and the cylinder.

He untied his kerchief and handed it to me.

I wrapped it tightly around the finger.

"You're supposed to fire lead at the Yankees, not at

your own fingertips," Anderson said as he placed the revolver in my belt. "But I suppose if you must give them a
finger, that is the one to load."

Another round of guffaws followed, and the pain of
being singled out for my stupidity was nearly as keen as
that which I felt throbbing, in time with my beating
heart, in my right hand.

"Look here," he said. "I'm not trying to be unkind,
but you will either get the hang of this—or it will get the
hang of you. Try not to be such a dingus."

10

Journalism in Missouri

INGUS. AS MUCH as I hated it, the name stuck. My left hand healed and caused me no permanent disability except embarrassment. Later I would make up an explanation for people who asked about the silly nickname, some improbable story about how I had pinched off the end of the finger while cleaning my revolver, because the truth was just too painful for a teenager to admit. But for Anderson and his boys in the summer of 1864, the only name I had was Dingus.

Although we were constantly on the move and supplies were short, if you had to be in the bush in Missouri, summer was the time. We were sometimes hungry, but never were we in danger of starvation, because even if we were out of the range of a sympathetic farmer, the woods offered abundant sustenance for those who knew what to look for—wild berries, sassafras tea, small game, and fish if you were near a creek. The things we were likely to be short of included horseshoes and nails, percussion caps, and lead. These things were under control of the provost marshals, and were sold only with their permission, and then only by merchants who were known to be loyal to the Union. Most of our clothes were stolen from the Yankees, and those among us who refused to wear blue stuck with homespun.

Anderson seemed to pick up enthusiasm as the summer went along, and our schedule of ambush and robbery intensified. We regularly tore up rail lines, downed telegraph wires, robbed coaches, and even managed to capture—or at least put a scare into her pilot—the occasional riverboat on the Missouri or one of her deeper tributaries. We never equaled the devastation Quantrell had wrought at Lawrence, but we managed to keep the Yankees busy chasing us.

During this time Anderson entertained himself by firing off letters to the newspapers, and every time we paid a visit to any outpost of civilization that wasn't actively engaged in shooting back, he would scour the town for the most recent papers. Like most psychopaths, he loved to see his name in print, and the only thing that disappointed him more than a disapproving editorial was to find himself not mentioned at all. After securing the latest editions, he would set up a few wooden chairs in the street, prop his boots on a barrel or whatever else was handy, and light a cigar. Then he would direct his little subordinate, Archie Clement, to read to him the latest news about himself.

The boys, of course, would listen as well.

He was holding just such a court in the middle of the only street in the tiny community of Bethlehem in central Missouri while Archie read to him the most recent editorial from the local paper. Now, newspapering had always been a wild thing on the frontier, but during the war it was an enterprise that only a masochist could love. No matter what you printed, no matter whose side you were on, you were liable to trigger a psychotic rage in at least half your readers. Getting your office burned and all your type dumped into the nearest river was the least you could expect. In the case of the poor editor of the *Bethlehem Bugle*, he must have been positively suicidal.

" 'William Andersen and his ilk are nothing more than common murderers and thieves,' " Archie read. " 'The ambush of the mail coach on the telegraph road, and the massacre of a score of Union soldiers, is the action of a man of such low character that we cannot print the term that accurately describes him. To do so would malign the entire male population of dogs.' "

Archie paused after that last bit.

"They've spelled your name wrong, Bill. With an s-e-n."

"God damn those Yankee bastards," Anderson stormed. "Go on."

"But, Bill—"

"Do it."

Archie cleared his throat and continued.

" 'We urge all citizens of the city of Bethlehem and beyond to take up arms against this scourge. If he and his men appear at your doorstep, do not hesitate to shoot them. You would do no less if any vicious animal threatened the safety of you, your family, and your property. And, we assure you, there is no more vicious animal loose in the wilderness of Missouri than William Andersen and his band of rascals.' "

Archie put down the newspaper.

"That's it, Bill."

Anderson drew a cigar from the pocket of his jacket. He stuck it in the corner of his mouth, struck a match on the heel of his boot, and lit it.

"What's this editor's name?" he asked.

Archie leafed through the newspaper.

"Zucker," Archie said. "J. P. Zucker."

"Bring him to me."

Archie saluted and trotted off.

Two of the boys went with him, and one of them had a coil of rope over his shoulder.

The print shop was down the street. The door was locked, but Archie and the others kicked it off its hinges. There followed shouting, and the sound of a scuffle, and then Archie burst back through the door with a firm grip on one end of the rope. At the other end, with a noose around his neck and his hands tied behind his back, was the editor.

Archie led him over and forced him down in the dirt in front of where Anderson was sitting. The man seemed old to me, although I reckon now he was only thirty, and he wore a vest and a white shirt with the sleeves rolled up. The man's hands and forearms were smudged with ink, and his eyes were weak and his complexion was pale, as if he seldom saw the sunlight.

One of the boys had returned from the print shop with a bottle of whiskey in his hand, which he threw in Anderson's direction. Anderson reached out and snatched it before it hit the ground.

"Are you Zucker?" he asked.

The man nodded.

"Get him a chair," Anderson said as he uncorked the bottle with his teeth. "Do you drink this stuff?"

"I'm a printer, ain't I?"

"Get us some cups."

While a chair was found for the unlucky editor, Archie produced a pair of tin cups. He filled each of them with whiskey.

"To your health," Anderson said.

The man was no stranger to irony, and gave a little groan at this, but he took the cup anyway. He took a big swig of it before returning his gaze to Anderson.

"You know who I am?"

"They call you Bloody Bill."

"My name is William Anderson. Anderson with an s-o-n. I read your piece," he said.

"Well, I reckon you didn't want to discuss the line rates."

"I was disturbed by your accusations," he said. "Apparently, your readers were as well. I see none of them rushing into the street to defend you."

"Goddamned cowards," Zucker muttered.

"Perhaps you would honor me with an opportunity to reply."

"What?"

"I want to answer your charges," Anderson said. "In your next edition."

"You're not going to kill me?"

"How can I do that and still have my reply printed in your newspaper?" Anderson grinned. "No, I'm not going to kill you. I'm going to show you that I know how to respond like a gentleman to these charges. Do you have some paper to take this down?"

"You'd like to dictate?"

"Is that a problem?"

"No," Zucker said slowly, "I guess not."

Zucker rummaged in his pockets and unfolded a wrinkled sheet of paper, then found the pencil behind his ear. He licked the tip of it and smoothed the paper on his knee before nodding.

Anderson tipped back in his chair and placed his hands behind his head.

"Mr. Editor," he began. "I see by reading your paper that you advocate a policy of the citizens taking up arms to defend their persons and their property against me. Sir, you are only asking them to sign their own death warrants. Do you—"

"Just a moment," Zucker said, trying to catch up.

"How does that sound so far?" Anderson asked.

"Damn good," Archie said. "Go to it, Bill."

"Okay, let's see," Anderson said, then cleared his throat. "Ahem. Do you not realize, sir, that you have the best and most noble of Missouri's sons to contend with? Ask your true citizens of Missouri who are acquainted with me if ever I robbed them, or harmed their persons, or mistreated them in any way. All those that speak the truth will say nay, never. Then who do you need protection from?

"I will tell you. There are bandits and thieves loose in the Missouri community, and they are not among my command. They do not belong to any organized band, but hold only to their individual selves and self-interests. They are just afraid of me, as they are the Federals, and I will help rid the community of them. They are not friends of mine. I have done all that language can do to stop these thefts, and now I will see what force can do."

Anderson paused here, drained the cup of whiskey, and let Zucker catch up.

"But listen to me, fellow citizens," Anderson went on. He was really getting warmed up now. "Do not obey this call to arms against me, for if you do, your lives will be forfeit. If you proclaim to be in arms against the guerrillas, I will kill you. I will hunt you down like wolves and murder you. The Federals cannot help you. Twenty-five of my men can whip any number you can get together, because my men are regulars of three seasons in the field, and are armed with from two to four pistols and Sharps rifles.

"I lived in Kansas when this war commenced and sought to fight for my country, not to steal from it. Because I would not fight the people of Missouri, the Yankees sought my life but failed to get me. They murdered my father, destroyed all my property, and have since that time murdered one of my sisters and kept the other two in jail for twelve months."

He stopped to take a breath, and Zucker raced to catch up. When he resumed, he was shouting:

"I have not fully glutted myself upon vengeance, although I have killed many. I am a guerrilla. Take up arms against me and I will kill you for being fools. And I will have to resort to abusing your ladies if you do not stop imprisoning ours. I will kidnap them from their beds in the dead of night, strip them of their nightclothes, tie them by the neck in the brush, and starve them until—"

"Captain," Archie said.

"Just a minute."

"*Bill,*" Archie said, and placed a hand on his shoulder. "This was supposed to be a gentleman's response, remember?"

"Right," Anderson said. "Well, it needs a little editing. Look here, Zucker, just strike that last part. Ahem. Let me finish now."

Anderson ran a hand over his beard.

"Young men, leave your mothers and fight for Missouri. Let them know that Missouri's sons will not be trampled under. Act carefully, for my eyes are upon you. Signed, W. Anderson, Commanding, First Kansas Guerrillas."

This last was greeted by profound silence.

"What was that?" one of the boys asked.

His name was Swisby, and although he was the only one who said anything, he really was speaking for the rest of us. He was a good fighter and one of the most level-headed of the bunch, which in a way was too bad. He would be dead within the month.

"You didn't know that was the official name of our outfit?" Anderson scoffed. "Hell, you knew I was from

Kansas. What else are we going to call ourselves?"

"We can call ourselves anything we like," Oscar Swisby replied. "We don't have an official name. That's what makes us guerrillas. But to call ourselves a *Kansas* outfit? I'm no goddamned abolitionist sandcutter, that's for sure."

"I don't remember asking your advice on how to run this command," Anderson fumed. He was getting increasingly agitated, and his hands were dancing among the butts of the revolvers that bristled at his belt and from his jacket pockets.

Swisby jammed his thumbs in his belt, his fingers splayed, and looked incredulously at Anderson.

"You're crazy," he said.

"Crazy like a chicken-eatin' fox," Anderson said.

Swisby shook his head and walked sadly away.

"You got all that?" Anderson asked.

Zucker nodded.

"Outstanding," Anderson said, and slapped him on the back. The blow nearly knocked Zucker off his chair. "Now, you get right to work setting that in type for next week's edition, and maybe we won't burn your shop to the ground, scatter your type over the better part of three acres, and stuff your mouth with your own product and leave you to rot where your kin will never find your body."

Zucker folded the piece of paper, put it in his vest pocket, and got unsteadily to his feet. He thanked Anderson for sharing his own whiskey, returned the cup, then began to walk off.

"And one more thing," Anderson shouted after him. "Make damn sure you spell my name right this time."

11

Trapping the Beast

FOR THE NEXT couple of weeks things went on pretty much the same, with us skulking around and finding whatever targets of opportunity presented themselves. The campaign wasn't exactly organized, and whenever somebody like Swisby would point out to Bloody Bill the questionable military benefit of scaring newspaper editors and ambushing the odd detail, Anderson would rant and rave about how the randomness embodied the very genius of his approach, because the Federals would never know where we were going to hit next.

I had lived through my first baptism of fire, and had managed to get saddled with that ridiculous nickname, but had yet to prove my worth as a soldier. To others I allowed as how I was eager to get into our next real scrap, but secretly I was worried that I would do something stupid again—or, worse, allow my fear to betray me. The good thing was that I wouldn't have to worry long about it.

The day after the incident with the newspaper editor we crossed the Missouri River. Our strength had diminished to twenty or so, which was not unusual; many of the boys would grow restless and return briefly to their homes, while others would form temporary associations and go on plundering expeditions of their own. They would be back after a time. Those who stayed numbered among the core of Anderson's command, such as Archie Clement, or those whose homes were too far away or too dangerous to visit, like me. Also, my reputation as a dingus may have discouraged many of the boys from inviting me to ride with them.

Nearly all of those who remained wore the uniforms that had been stripped from the bodies of our enemies, and many of those who saw us coming mistook us for Federals. I, however, refused to wear blue. The memory of the whipping by men wearing similar uniforms was still too fresh in my memory.

As we approached the town of Wankeda, we stopped at selected farms, where Anderson questioned the men about their loyalties. He apparently had some kind of list that was provided to him by one of the local boys. Because the strangers thought we were Federal cavalry, they all proclaimed their loyalty to the Union, and many said they had served in the state militia. Anderson would nod, seem satisfied with their answers, and then shoot them dead—except for one man, who suspected what was up and cursed Anderson. His throat was slit from ear to ear by Little Archie Clement. Another man changed his story when they draped a rope around his neck, and although he protested his loyalty to the South, Anderson ordered him hanged.

"String him up," Anderson said. "God damn his little soul, he's a Dutchman anyway."

Later we found out he was telling the truth.

If all of this sounds horrible to relate, then you can imagine what it was like to watch the gruesome spectacle. There was no soldiering to it, and I will leave to your imagination the grief of the families. At the time I told myself it was revenge, that we were giving back as good as we had got, and that these men were the enemy. I didn't think too hard about it at the time it was happening, partly because I had watched and did nothing, partly because I was scared to death of Anderson and his little murderer, and partly because at sixteen I had a hard time putting these things into words. But I knew in my heart what was right, even if I couldn't explain it to anybody, and it began eating at me something fierce.

Revenge has been strictly overrated.

I had felt a surge of excitement shoot through me when Anderson had questioned the first one, and I leaned forward in my saddle so I could hear every word, and witness the frightened look in the poor man's eyes, and then—*bang!*—he was sprawled on the ground with his wife beside him, and his brains scattered all over the front of her dress. My stomach flopped on me and I got sick and vomited over the side of my saddle, while Little Archie sneered at me and cooed in Anderson's bushy ear that "Dingus has no stomach for our work."

There I was, getting exactly what I had wanted in my fantasies after the Yankees whipped me and hung my pappy by the neck until he became an idiot. These weren't *the* soldiers, but they had been state militia, most of them, and the tables had been turned—here I was among the group of men to be feared and reckoned with. Yet there was only sorrow in it, and I played the part of the coward.

Revenge was a word that was tossed around mighty easily during the war, and it became the battle cry of the guerrillas. The burning of Lawrence and the killing of the hundred and fifty is a good example. But did any of those men and boys actually cause the collapse of the barracks in Kansas City? No. Hell, they weren't even *soldiers* of the other side. They were symbols. And that's the way it is with revenge, you're always taking your hatred out on somebody that stands for that hate, and hardly ever the person that did you the harm in the first place.

And the peculiar thing is that hatred had turned me— and every other boy that left home to join the guerrillas and seek revenge—into an exact copy of the thing I hated. I might as well have whipped myself and strung old Pappy up, because there was not one atom of difference.

So when the Lord says in the Good Book that vengeance is His, I reckon the old bastard was telling the truth. Because it just doesn't seem to work that well for human beings, despite all that "eye for an eye" stuff.

There you have the moral to this story. If you were looking for one, you need read no further. I knew this lesson at sixteen, but I refused to take it to heart. It probably won't have much of an influence on you either, unless you've lived it.

But I turned away from the truth.

Of course, if I hadn't, you wouldn't be reading this right now because you would never have heard of a lad called Jesse James because he would have thrown down his guns and went back to his home in Clay County and lived out the rest of his natural life in obscurity. The end.

But . . .

As I said, I couldn't put all of this into words at the time, but my heart just kept getting heavier and heavier. It got to the point where I wasn't feeling anything. The daily routine just got drearier and drearier.

Life in the bush is interesting to relate, but that's because you're discussing only the high points, and the rest of it is deadly dull and tiresome. Folks go "camping" now to remind themselves of what it's like to be outside, and for a day or two it's great fun, but if they had to do it every day, they would be desperate to find someplace they could call inside. The bush was like that, only with people shooting at you occasionally and about a third of your fellows sick at any one time.

But it is a human failing that you remember the times of high drama best—those times when you are in mortal danger, when you are fighting for your life and the lives of your fellows, and it is those times when you have cheated death that you feel most alive.

Truth to tell, those were about the only times I did feel alive during the war. And to that Anderson soon added something diabolical to the mix, something that few men and no teenager could deny; he added the aspect of robbery on a grand scale.

As we neared the community of Huntsville, the population was in a panic. Word had spread about the eight union men and the one mistake we had executed on the way. Those loyal to the Union left in droves, and wrote panicked letters to the Union commanders demanding that something be done about us. Our strength had swelled just to thirty-five by the time we reached Huntsville, which was the seat of Randolph County, but nary a regular soldier dared to challenge us.

We took the town by killing the only opposition—a lone Union sympathizer armed with a shotgun—and then robbed the bank by kicking down its doors. After hauling the paper money and the gold out in sacks, we then abused the other merchants. They had little cash money, but we satisfied ourselves with taking whatever else we wanted.

Anderson set up court as usual and announced that Huntsville was "his capital." He immediately began writing dispatches to the local newspapers about the victory. The secessionist faction came out of the woodwork, hoping to gain favor and share in the spoils.

The action at Huntsville submerged any lingering

doubts I may have had about our way of life. Money beat the living hell out of revenge. My reward was a pair of Colt navies to replace the damned old dragoon pistol, and a saddlebag stuffed full of greenbacks and a little gold. It was a modest amount, perhaps around a thousand dollars, but it was more money than I had ever seen at one time.

We left Huntsville after a few days. Our ranks had grown to more than a hundred, and now Anderson decided that we would hamper transportation. We attacked the steamboat *War Eagle* at Rocheport, then turned our wrath upon the North Missouri Railroad at Rennick, where we burned the depot.

We aimed to do the same at Allen, but was met by a stubborn group of local militia that refused to yield. It was kind of a shock, after having ridden unchecked for so long, to meet resistance of any kind. We didn't stay and fight, as they were soon reinforced by a trainload of Illinois cavalry. We withdrew down the Huntsville road—and waited.

The next day the militia and the Illinois troopers came looking for us. We ambushed them, and they scattered, but not before two of the troopers were killed. Anderson and Clement scalped both and left them in the middle of the road. It was gruesome to watch, especially because the little butcher did it with such relish, but I rationalized it with the fact that these men had been armed and were killed in battle. To one of them was pinned the message "You came to hunt bushwhackers. Now you are skelpt. Sincerely, Wm. Anderson."

We then made our way over to Shelby County, where we attacked the Hannibal and St. Joseph. We torched depots, pulled down telegraph lines, and ripped up track. Then we burned the wooden railway bridge over the Salt River, which was our biggest strategic victory of the

summer. It would take the Yankees a few months to replace the bridge, and in the meantime they had to trans-
fer troops around the broken span.

Now, I had participated in all of these events so far,
but had never found myself in any desperate fighting yet.
Mostly, it was a matter of riding like hell and yelling, or
engaging in a very brief confrontation with the enemy,
with a lot of looting and burning for good measure.

Then Anderson decided he wanted to capture a
locomotive.

So we ripped up a section of track, built a fire with
the ties, and draped the rails over it so they would heat up
and twist into unusable shapes. It was hard work, all with
pickaxes and sledges, and it took us the better part of an
afternoon to accomplish our task.

It made me homesick to think that near the western
end of the steel rails was my home in Clay County.[1] The
Hannibal and St. Joseph tracks ran to within three miles
of the farm, and I had often walked them as a boy, hunting rabbits and other game, and occasionally wondering
what life was like at the other end. It struck me as ironic
that I was now daydreaming in the other direction.

The section we had chosen was a slow turn around a
low hill, after making a gradual climb out of the river valley, which would make it impossible for the engineer of
the locomotive to spot the break in the tracks until it was
too late. The train would wreck, or at least be forced to a
dead stop. Then, if it wasn't too heavily defended, we
would swoop down to capture, plunder, and burn.

Anderson had posted a lookout on top of the hill to
watch for the train, and also to alert us if any patrols
should happen our way. We were about finished with the
track-wrecking job, when the picket comes whooping

---

[1] At the other end was Twain's hometown of Hannibal.

down the hill, shouting that he had seen black smoke above the trees on the other side of the valley. The train was coming.

We all mounted our horses and waited.

It was that time in the late afternoon when everything gets still, and we could hear the train as it chugged up the hill toward us. Then the train rounded the curve. Like all of the locomotives west of the Mississippi it was a "Prairie" configuration, with two large drive wheels on each side and small wheels in front and beneath the cab. It was pushing a flatcar in front of it, and the car was loaded with sandbags, and behind the sandbags was a little mountain howitzer and a half dozen soldiers with rifles. I could see the engineer's startled expression as he gawked out the window of the cab at the ruined track, the bonfire of ties and twisted steel, and us waiting beyond. The drive wheels squalled and showered sparks as he set the brake and attempted to slow the forward motion of the train.

The soldiers abandoned the car just before it plowed into the fiery barricade. The front truck of the flatcar burst through in a shower of sparks, then left the rails and buried itself in the shoulder of the road. It plowed through earth for several yards this way before the rear end of the flatcar twisted and then broke itself to pieces on the ramlike cowcatcher at the front of the locomotive.

The howitzer exploded, and a chunk of the breech was propelled gracefully through the air. It seemed like it was going in slow motion, but the force behind it became apparent when it landed on poor Swisby, killing horse and rider.

"Damn," Anderson muttered. "I fancied that gun."

Then the train ground to a stop with only the tiny front wheels of the locomotive hanging off the end of the track. The soldiers who had jumped off the flatcar were now clamoring to join their fellows in the cars behind the tender.

The engineer paused as he assessed the situation.

For a moment the locomotive crouched before us like a great black beast, and we could feel the thumping of its heart in time to the blossoms of smoke that rose from its ornate stack. Then it hissed like a dragon as hot steam shot from its jaws, and the drive wheels began to claw at the rails in reverse.

"Seize the cab!" Anderson shouted as he surged forward.

Along with a hundred other guerrillas, I dug my heels into my mount and followed. We began shooting wildly at the beast, and every shot was punctuated by the sound of lead smacking against the locomotive.

We swarmed around the slow-moving train while the engineer and the fireman ducked for cover. The troops in the boxcars threw open their doors and began to return fire, and they played hell with the guerrillas who were pursuing along the inside of the curve. A few of our boys were shot right out of the saddle, which discouraged the attack on that side.

Which, of course, was my side. I let the locomotive pass, then crossed over the tracks and resumed my assault from the other side. Although our boys who had Sharps were having some luck penetrating the locomotive boiler's water jacket, most of us might as well have been throwing rocks. A revolver was made for use against human beings and little else.

Also, the train was picking up speed. Anderson had failed to take into account the grade of the tracks as they came out of the valley, at least not when it came to chasing a locomotive back down. Already my horse was at a gallop, and pretty soon I would be forced into a run just to keep up.

Then I had an inspiration.

If I could only swing up into the cab, which appeared to be only slightly defended, I could single-handedly capture the train and maybe even rid myself of that horrible nickname.

So I spurred my horse and broke ahead of the others.

The tracks had straightened now, so I found myself riding close beside the locomotive to keep out of the sights of the infantry leaning out of the boxcars. The footing on the roadbed was not good, and my horse stumbled once, and the image of being ground to death beneath the wheels of the train flashed through my mind. So I stood in the saddle, grasped a piece of brass railing, then leaped over onto the side of the locomotive. Hot steam and scalding water were spewing from a dozen holes along the length of the boiler, and by the time I reached the edge of the cab, I felt nearly cooked.

At about this time some troopers, led by an officer, started making their way over the top of the tender. The train was now so far ahead of the guerrillas that they could offer me no covering fire, so I sent a couple of shots over their head to keep them down while I tried to climb through the side window of the cab.

I had one leg through the window when the fireman came at me with the flat end of the shovel they used to clear ashes out of the box. He busted me on the leg with it, and while I was thus distracted, the Yankee captain seized the opportunity to rush forward and try to kill me.

He made it to the front end of the tender, just yards away, and stood perched atop the swaying pile of kindling while he jammed the barrel of his revolver in my direction. The fireman crowded into the engineer's corner, while the engineer remained in his seat and continued to drive the train.

We banged away at each other until my gun was empty.

Miraculously, we were both still alive.

As I reached for my other revolver, I realized with a sickening feeling that it had already been spent during the first part of the attack on the train. My attention was still on my empty guns, when the captain fired once more with his navy.

At first I thought the fireman had whacked me in the chest with the shovel. The .36-caliber ball had struck me in the right breast, and I fell heavily against the side of the cab. Then the pain truly hit me, and it felt as if someone had impaled me with a very dull and very hot poker. My revolver dangled from the fingers of my right hand and then clattered to the steel floor.

"He's just a kid," the engineer exclaimed in surprise now that he was looking down at my face instead of at the barrel of my gun. "Take him back to stand trial, but don't kill him."

"My orders," the captain said, "are to execute guerrillas on the spot. He just got his trial."

I noticed now that his left arm was hanging oddly from his shoulder, and how the sleeve was wet with blood.

At least I had hit the sonuvabitch.

The captain put the bead of his revolver on my head.

I winced as the hammer snapped on a spent chamber.

His men were now clustering behind him, and I knew I had been spared by a miracle, but had only a moment to get clear of this Yankee shooting gallery.

I lurched to my feet and blindly jumped from the cab.

Now, that's where I'm supposed to leave it, right? End on a moment of suspense. Keep you just enough in the dark so you'll rush out to buy the next installment, or at least turn to the next chapter to see what happens next. At least, that's how the hacks do it who write the dime novels and penny dreadfuls.

Well, the suspense is hardly warranted.

The locomotive had reached the trestle over the creek at the edge of the valley, and I fell from the cab and landed in shallow water and mud at the edge of the marshy bank. I was buried so deep that I would have suffocated if a group of my fellows, who had been following, had not hauled me out. Most believed I would die, although a few argued on my behalf, so I was eventually taken to a nearby farm, where a family of sympathetic strangers named Rudd cared for me until I recovered.

The pistol ball had lodged in my rib cage—where it is still—and despite the amount of pain it caused, it had not struck anything vital. Although I was grateful for their care, life at the farm was pretty dismal, and there was no pretty girl to nurse me back to health, as you may have anticipated.

12

Centralia

THE RUDDS WERE initiates of a secret society known as the Knights of the Golden Circle and were always jabbering in code language and giving secret signs to one another. They kept talking about the revolution that was coming, and they would laugh among themselves about which neighbors they would hang first, but I never saw anything that made me believe it would happen. None of it made much sense, especially since John Rudd was damned near eighty and his two boys seemed nearly as old. When I asked them about it, they would just smile and say that it was a shame I wasn't a member of their castle—that's what they called their lodges—because if they told me their secrets, they would have sworn a blood oath to kill me. But they were quick to tell me not to worry, because they would make sure I was spared when the revolt came, just because I had been fighting on God's side.

That was my cue to smile sweetly and say "thank you," even though I knew they were as crazy as pet raccoons. For one thing, the trio of old geezers didn't own a pistol among them. For another, I couldn't see how there was any money to be made in the scheme, so I didn't think folks would be much interested. The Yankees, for example, had made the military occupations of Missouri extremely profitable for the provost marshals and others who enforced the law; and the guerrillas had made things equally attractive, through sharing the spoils, for those willing to risk death to fight the Yankees. The game of belonging to a secret society, however, seemed to be its own reward, with no cash involved.

But most folks seem to be suckers for a conspiracy, especially when they feel they're among the enlightened. Thousands and thousands of people in Missouri belonged to the Golden Circle or a similar organization—the Order of American Knights, for example, or the Sons of Liberty—but they all seemed to be just poor white trash. They'd never had any power in their lives, they were afraid to pick up a gun and fight in earnest, but they could play-act and convince themselves of how much nobler they were than their neighbors, somehow.

The Yankees never could keep the organizations straight, and they tended to regard all of the flavors—from Copperheads and Peace Democrats to the Sons and the American Knights—as basically the same. Which is to say, traitorous.

The Golden Circle had the best pedigree because its roots stretched all the way back to William Walker and his Immortals. They had briefly, in the 1850s, seized Nicaragua as a sort of stepping-stone to Central America. Their goal was to take control of Cuba as well and turn the Gulf of Mexico into a sort of "southern pond," and avoid the cumbersome compromises that had turned the admission of every new state into a tug-of-war between the abolitionists and the slaveholders. Only, the Immortals proved to be a poorly named bunch. After failing to hold the country, Walker and most of his men were taken out on the beach and shot.

Still, it was a pretty dream.

I reckon that somewhere the Knights of the Golden Circle are still meeting, right here in the twentieth century, just waiting for the revolt and their chance to turn to their neighbors—at least the ones they spared—and say, "I told you so."

So my seventeenth birthday passed while I was imprisoned by these lunatics. It was late September before I was well enough to ride again, but as soon as I could climb into a saddle without fainting from the pain, I gave the Rudds a few pieces of gold for their trouble and took my leave.

By following the grapevine I found Anderson camped not far away in Boone County, on land owned by a wealthy farmer named Singleton. It seems that Singleton had always been a Southern sympathizer, but of late had turned absolutely rabid because of the treatment his wife had received when the local militia came to visit. Not only had they ruined the family's dinner by feeding it to the dogs, but they had piled their boots and their guns on Mrs. Singleton's bed.

It seems a minor offense now, considering the range of things that men with guns are capable of, but in those far-off days of 1864, such behavior seemed outrageous.

So despite the fact that Anderson was a murderous lunatic, he was more than welcomed at the Singleton farm, as were the commands of George Todd and John Thrailkill. All told, there were two hundred and fifty guerrillas camped on the farm. Now, it may seem like a bold move for Singleton to offer us accommodations, but what choice did he really have? Two hundred and fifty guerrillas could pretty well sleep where they wanted.

The guerrillas were together in such unusual force because we had been asked to create a diversion for old

Sterling Price's "invasion" of Missouri. Price, a general in the Confederate Army, was counting on recruiting fresh troops as he made his way up from Arkansas. Things had started bright enough for Old Pap, as he was called, because he was in command of twelve thousand men. But he failed to take the state capitol when he had the chance, just as he had declined St. Louis. By October he would be hounded all the way to the Kansas border, where he would become the commander of an army of refugees who carried their worldly possessions in two-wheeled carts. They would expect Price to protect them, but the Yankees would snip at their heels all the way to the Indian Nations.

But back in September we didn't know things would turn out so badly.

Anderson and the others took their orders seriously, and they had engaged in some of the wildest action of the war during my absence. They had sacked towns, ambushed steamboats, looted banks, burned courthouses, and in one instance had captured an entire Yankee garrison without firing a shot. At one point during my recuperation, Anderson and his men had even raided in Clay County.

Quantrell had also returned to the field during my absence, and I learned from others that my brother Buck was still alive and under his command. By the time I joined the boys on the Singleton farm, however, Buck was gone. Quantrell had sought his own way again after Anderson led a disastrous assault on a fortified brick courthouse at Fayette in Howard County, which left more than a dozen guerrillas dead and many more wounded. It was Quantrell's philosophy that you didn't attack anything that wouldn't burn.

When I reported to Anderson, he hardly blinked.

"Dingus," he said. "Back for more?"

"Yes, Captain," I managed to say.

"How did you like being shot?" he asked.

"If it's all the same," I said, "I would rather be on the other end of the gun."

"Consider it part of your education," Anderson said.

The next day Bloody Bill was up before dawn and ranting about the lack of current newspapers. Inactivity of any kind made him wild with impatience, and the sheer number of men camped on the farm seemed to agitate him in some strange way. He raved that he couldn't listen to his own thoughts with so much humanity milling about, and that he wished everybody would just take a moment and let their minds go blank so he could have some peace. He spent the next quarter of an hour with his fists pressed against his ears, but that apparently offered no relief. Now, I don't know what he was hearing, because the camp was as silent as a church, but it must not have been pleasant, judging from the look on his face.

"Get up, Dingus," he shouted as he kicked the bottoms of my feet to get me out from under my blanket. "Let's go see what the St. Louis press is saying about Captain Anderson today!"

He ordered around thirty of us to mount up and accompany him to the nearest town, which lay four miles to the north. It was chilly, and my body ached, but dutifully I rose and pulled on my boots.

The sun was not far above the horizon when we rode into Centralia. It was a tiny community that had sprung up around the North Missouri Railroad a few years before, and the depot was the center of town. With the exception of a pack of dogs that lurked in the alleys and fought over scraps, we were the only living things moving.

Anderson stood in the saddle and took a look around.

"This will never do!" he roared as he pulled his pistols and began shooting into the air. "Come on, boys, let's wake these Yankee sonsabitches up!"

While Little Archie Clement led a detail to tear down the telegraph wires, another group of boys began smashing the windows of the few shops that fronted the main road. It wasn't long before they found a pair of prizes that made them whoop and holler with joy—a crate of boots and a barrel of whiskey.

The boots were distributed to the dozen nearest guerrillas, and they proudly hung them over the necks of their horses. Meanwhile, the lid of the barrel of whiskey was knocked in. Everyone clustered around, dipped their tin cups into the amber liquid, and greedily slurped it down.

The poor storekeeper and his wife stumbled down from their loft to make a formal complaint about the confiscation of his goods. The boys were more interested in the woman than they were in the merchant, however, and soon they were passing her from one to another and begging affection.

Now, I have since noticed that things are likely to go to hell quick when you combine an armed bunch of men with a quantity of liquor.

The treatment of the wife became increasingly rough. At no point did it appear that she was about to be raped, but the boys obviously thought they were repaying the treatment of the Singleton woman by the militia. When the husband objected even more strenuously and challenged the boys to fistfight to protect her honor, somebody pulled a pistol and shot him dead. This put a damper on things, so the woman was released. She retreated back upstairs, weeping and calling "murder" as she went.

The drunken guerrillas then set the depot on fire.

Anderson threw a fit when he realized the building

had been ignited before he had a chance to scour it for a St. Louis newspaper, and he had a brief argument with the arsonists in which he urged them to dash back inside and take a quick look around before the flames claimed all.

None would volunteer.

Anderson and Little Archie then marched off, looking for breakfast. He found it too. He set up court in the dining room of Sneeds Hotel, smoking cigars, reading old newspapers, and speculating on just what Pap Price was up to at that very moment.

The drinking and rioting continued for the next couple of hours. I had not acquired a taste for spirits, so I remained clearheaded and contented myself instead with raiding the storefronts for meats, bread, and cheese. I didn't mind stealing food, but my appetite didn't run to forcing enemy women to prepare it at gunpoint.

Just as things were lagging a bit, the stagecoach from Columbia rattled in. Clement and the others had quite a bit of sport robbing the passengers and asking them, while waving a pistol in their faces, about their loyalties.

One man in particular was so eloquent in his support for the Confederacy that everybody stopped their looting just to listen to him. He said he was a local farmer, although he looked like he'd never worked a day in his life. But he gave this speech about the South's right to govern itself, and about how all of us boys were patriots. He called us the "sons of the south" and declared that someday little children would read about us in the history books, just like George Washington and Thomas Paine and Paul Revere.

Clement let him go, just on principle. He bid us farewell and good luck, then walked away just like he was royalty. We should have figured him for a politician. Later somebody told us he was a United States congressman by the name of Rollins.

Along about noon, a train whistle alerted us that we were about to have visitors.

Anderson came out of the hotel and told us all to hide. The boys had already made a barricade by piling ties and other debris on the rails.

The engineer must have spotted the smoke from the burning depot, because the train came barreling in from the east and made no indication that it was prepared to stop. He hadn't counted on the barricade, however, and he threw on the brakes just in time to avoid a horrible wreck.

The boys jumped up and started shooting the windows out of the cars. As the passengers ran out, we robbed them. Among them were twenty-six Federal soldiers. They were all Missouri boys, and they were on furlough from Sherman in Georgia. All of them were unarmed.

I was sorry for them the instant I saw them. I don't know why that engineer didn't throw his locomotive in reverse and get out of there when we started shooting, but I suppose there may have been another train behind them. If he had known what was to come, surely he would have taken the risk.

Clement made them line up, then he posted guards on either side and marched them down the platform. He made them stand at attention in the middle of the street while he explained that we needed their uniforms.

The soldiers looked fresh, even to me. Even the youngest of our guerrillas had a red-eyed, rawboned look that came from life outside. But these fellows looked positively pink, and they glanced at one another out of the corners of their eyes while wondering what to do.

"Well, what are you waiting for?" Clement bellowed. "Strip!"

They climbed out of their uniforms.

Some of them had drawers on underneath, but most

of them now stood as naked as the day they were born. There was something about the act of shedding their uniforms that had turned these men into something other than human beings. A naked person in public is at once removed from society, and is ordinarily the subject of amusement. After all, incongruity is the soul of humor. But there was nothing funny about the men in the middle of the road; for as soon as I saw them standing there, all pink and helpless, I knew that Clement was going to kill them.

Now, I have considered my next statement for the better part of an hour, without knowing how to proceed. Damn your questions! When I began this narrative, it did not occur to me that the thread of it would wind around to eventually trap me within a web created by my own words. Others have never been so impertinent as to subject me to a cross-examination of my actions during the war. Ordinarily, I would lie or claim a weakness of memory, but never before have I stood so close to the threshold of eternity. Yes, you're right. With every breath we all inch a little closer to that threshold, though we never admit it, no matter what our age. Here, only truth will do.

It would be my fondest wish to report that I stood up to the little bastard and protested the treatment of these prisoners. But I did nothing.

Anderson came out to inspect the prisoners. He was mounted, which made the scene even more bizarre. His scalps were swinging from the bridle. He was smoking a cigar. He was enjoying himself.

"What a sorry-looking bunch of rabbits," he commented.

"Yes, Captain," Clement chirped. "They are indeed."

"Are there any officers in the bunch?" Anderson asked.

"I don't recall, sir," Clement said.

"Well, it's damned difficult to tell now."

"Are any of you officers?" Clement shouted as he walked down the line. "No officers? Are there any non-commissioned officers among you?"

The line seemed to stir a bit.

"Well?" Clement bellowed.

One of the older men set his jaw and stepped forward. He was a big, ruddy-faced man with a shock of red hair and a constellation of freckles across his barrel chest.

"Sir," he said. His voice was steady, his bearing was military, and I could not help but admire his calm. "Thomas Goodman, sergeant, Missouri Engineers."

"Cut him out," Anderson said.

Clement grabbed him by the hair of the head.

"If you please," Goodman said, and brushed the hand away. He stepped away from the line, toward Anderson. "Sir, might I have a word before you shoot me?"

"If you wish," Anderson said.

"May I have the honor of knowing whom I address?"

Anderson smiled. He loved saying his name.

"Of course," he said. "Perhaps you've heard of me. I am William Anderson, guerrilla." With a flourish, he doffed his hat and leaned low over his horse's neck.

"In exchange for myself, I would ask that you release the others," Goodman pleaded. "Most of them are just boys, and have seen little action. As such, they pose no threat to you."

"You're in no position to ask anything," Anderson said as he replaced his hat. "Also, you may be interested to know that I don't intend to kill you. Instead, I intend to make you my guest for an indeterminate period. But let me ask you this, Sergeant. Do you know what penalty your army imposes on guerrillas captured in the field?"

Goodman nodded.

"Your fellows will be treated with the same consideration," Anderson said.

"Then damn you to hell," Goodman said.

"Surely I am," Anderson replied.

Goodman was led away.

"Lieutenant," Anderson called. "Muster out the troops."

Clement grinned, pulled both of his revolvers from his belt, and began firing into the prisoners. Anderson and most of the boys joined in. One of the Federals broke from the line and managed to duck beneath the wooden freight dock in front of the smoldering depot. After Clement made sure that all the others were dead by walking among them and firing a bullet into each of their skulls, the freight dock was doused with coal oil and set ablaze. The survivor was shot when he could stand the flames no more and bolted from his hiding place.

Goodman was put on a horse and his feet were tied beneath him so he couldn't escape.

Before leaving Centralia, the tracks in front of the train were cleared. Anderson finally had his train, so he decided to have some sport with it. First, he ordered all the cars set on fire. Then, personally, he tied the whistle down and opened the throttle.

The train looked like an apparition from hell as it left Centralia behind with its whistle screaming and all of the rolling stock on fire. It disappeared down the tracks to the west, leaving a greasy black smudge behind in the sky behind it.

As soon as my boots touched the soil of the Singleton farm, somebody stuck a pistol in the small of my back and told me in a low voice not to move.

"Shoot or shut the hell up," I said while continuing to tend to my horse.

"Well, I reckon I'll have to shut up, because I sure as hell don't want to plug my little brother in the kidneys," the voice replied.

It was Frank. He spun me around, knocked my hat off, then got me in a bear hug around the neck. He was taller and thinner than I had remembered, his hair was nearly as long as a girl's, and he hadn't shaved in at least a week. He was dressed in a mud-spattered jacket that had been gray at one time, and it was cinched with a broad belt that carried two Remingtons and a big Arkansas-style hunting knife.

I picked up my hat and smiled. It was the first time I'd really smiled in weeks, and my face was so tight that it felt like my cheeks were going to crack.

"Buck, I'd never thought I'd say this, it's good to see you."

"Some of the boys tell me you got shot."

"Yeah, but it wasn't so bad. I lived."

"And that nickname—"

"They told you about that, huh?"

"Lemme see your finger," Frank said, and grabbed my left hand. "I'll be damned, Horatio, it is true. Come over here and look at this thing."

He pulled one of his friends over to examine the hand. I jerked it back after they had gawked at it for a while.

"Let me introduce you fellows," Frank said. "Horatio, I want you to meet my little brother, Jesse Woodson James, better known to his comrades as Dingus. Jesse, I want you to meet Henry Williams."

"Frank calls me Horatio for some damned reason," Williams said as we clasped hands together.

Williams was a big blond giant with an easy grin.

"What are you doing over here?" I asked. "You haven't deserted Quantrell, have you?"

"Charley's not far behind," Frank said. "He sent us forward to scout out the situation here at the farm, and to see what Bloody Bill and the other chieftains were up to. I swear, our leaders are as vain as a pack of old ladies."

"Any news from home?" I asked.

"Things are tough, but Mother is still ornery as ever and holding her own," Frank said. "John Thomas is getting big, and our sisters are turning pretty."

"You were there?"

"Once, last month, when Quantrell swung up north and hid in the Sni-a-bar timber. Came and went in the middle of the night. Mother asked about you, but of course I had no idea that you'd been shot. Where'd you get it?"

"Right here," I said, and indicated the spot on my chest.

Frank poked at it, and I flinched.

"Still sore, huh?"

"And they say you're the smart one," I said. "Had a toe-to-toe with a Yankee captain, and he won."

"Did Bloody Bill promote you?"

"Who can tell?" I snorted. "He calls me 'lieutenant' every now and then, but he calls everybody that. There are no private soldiers in this command, it's all officers. I reckon it's because you can't consider yourself a knight of the bush if you're a common soldier. So, all ranks below lieutenant are discouraged. What's your rank?"

"Lieutenant," Frank said.

"See there? You have the system too."

"No, ours is a little more elaborate," Frank said. "We also have scouts and aides-de-camp."

"Damn," I said. "All we need are squires—"

"—like Sancho Panza."

"I don't know him," I said. "But what about your buddy, Cole Younger? Some of the boys were telling me you've formed a fast friendship with that one. You fellows are some sort of famous, and that's saying something about a group that considers themselves all heroes."

"Oh, Bud Younger," Frank said. "He's a good man. His folks are from Harrisonville down in Cass County, on the border, and they had it even worse than we did. He's the only person I've found that can talk books with me in the whole outfit, and he's a scrapper to boot."

"Will he be along?"

"No, they sent him out to Colorado on some kind of secret detail."

"Well, I wish I was with him right now," I said. "You boys had better get yourselves ready for a fight if you're going to stay here. I was with Bloody Bill over at Centralia this morning. We were looking for newspapers, but . . ."

"What's wrong?" Frank asked. "Your eyes still bothering you?"

"All the time," I said, and rubbed them with my palms.

"Don't do that," Frank said, and brushed my hands away. "You'll just make 'em worse."

"Buck, we lined up a bunch of Federals this morning and shot them down. But the Yankees are going to call it a massacre, seeing as how these soldier boys were unarmed, and I'll be damned if they won't be calling it right."

"Perhaps they had it coming," Frank said. "This is war."

"I've got nothing else to compare it to, so I'll take your word," I said. "But whatever you call it, the Yankees aren't going to swallow this one very easily. They'll be coming after us for sure, and damned quick."

"Let 'em come," Frank said.

"Yeah," Williams echoed. "Let 'em."

"They can't be crazy enough to try to take us here."

"There were only thirty of us in town this morning," I said. "They may think that's all they're chasing. How would they know that just about every guerrilla in central Missouri is camped four miles away?"

At four o'clock that afternoon a company of Federals led by Ave Johnston entered Centralia and discovered the devil's handiwork. Learning that the destruction had been wrought by only thirty men, he left half his command behind to guard the town and took out after us.

On the road outside Centralia, Johnston spotted ten guerrillas retreating before him. Encouraged, the major gave chase. When they topped a small hill at the edge of the Singleton farm, they saw below them more than two hundred wildcats standing beside their horses, waiting.

Anderson, of course, had posted the ten riders to lure the troops into an ambush. When they came racing back, we knew it was time to get ready to fight, so we formed a rough line with our backs to the timber. When we met the enemy, there wasn't a hundred yards between us.

Major Johnston was a good-looking man with a full beard, and he sat as straight as a ramrod in the saddle as he gazed down upon us. He had perhaps seventy men around him. They were mounted, but we knew immediately they were infantry. We weren't close enough to really make out the piping on their uniforms, but we could clearly see that all of them carried cumbersome single-shot rifles.

The men looked panicked, and more than a couple of them turned their horses to run, but Johnston pulled his pistol from his flap holster and commanded them to stop. His sergeants enforced the order. Then he slowly dismounted, withdrew his sword, and rammed it into the earth. He then sent the horses to the rear while his men formed a regulation line.

Things had gotten awfully quiet on our side, but the silence was broken when somebody said rather loudly what all the rest of us were thinking: "God help them, the fools are going to fight us on foot."

Johnston may have reasoned that his men had a better chance on the ground, where they had been trained to fight. And, as an infantry commander, his instinct would have told him to hug the high ground. Besides, you can't really fire one of those long single-shot Enfields from the back of a horse, at least not with any accuracy, and once you did, there was no hope of reloading without getting off the horse again. On foot, his men probably could manage three rounds a minute if they'd paid attention to their training.

But what he was missing was the most obvious thing, and that was the numbers against him. To me, the choice would have been between to stay and have everybody die fighting, or to make a run for town and hope for the best. Chances are that at least some of the men would have made it. But I reckon the major just assumed they were all going to die, no matter what.

Frank and Horatio and I were all together in the center of the line. As we mounted up, Frank shook his head. The high ground really didn't matter to us—the things that frustrated us guerrillas the most were structures, or any kind of cover where the enemy could snipe at us without being seen. But these boys were unprotected.

"I suppose they'll call this another massacre," he told me. "But they came here looking for a fight. They have guns pointing at us. What are we to supposed do, cordially decline the invitation until they've erected a earthworks?"

"I reckon not," I said.

Despite the odds in our favor, I wasn't feeling too talkative just then, because I was staring at the business ends of those rifles. An Enfield is an awkward and heavy weapon, as I've said, but it fires a humongous saboted bullet called a minié ball. They take a charge of powder that is about the size of your little finger. Their bores are nearly seven tenths of an inch across, and because they have long rifled barrels, these guns are accurate and consequently lethal at four or five times the range of a pistol. Enfields, and copies of them, were the ubiquitous weapon of the infantryman on both sides.

This was the first time I had stared at a line that bristled with Enfields, and I knew we would have to close the distance between us pretty damned quick. Also, I was feeling more than a little superstitious. In my mind was the thought that because of the events of that morning, God may have put my name on one of those ugly little saboted missiles waiting to be fired.

So I offered up a silent prayer for deliverance. If God couldn't manage that, I negotiated, then I would settle for just a little bit of luck.

Then Anderson let out a rebel yell, and we all surged forward.

Right off, the infantry let loose with a volley. I guess their plan was to take out as many of us as possible while our pistols were still out of range, and then reload before we were upon them. But most of that first volley sailed over our heads, because they hadn't compensated for shooting downward.

As we raced up the hill we could see most of them frantically attempting to reload by biting the ends from their paper cartridges and ramming them down the barrels. Some of them were so scared out of their wits, however, that they threw down their rifles and fell to their knees. Still others had saved their shots until we were close enough to better their chances of hitting a moving target.

One of these marksmen hit Henry Williams in the head, and he flew from the saddle as if kicked by a horse, and I felt doubly sorry because he spilled his brains all over Frank's leg as he fell.

Then we were upon them, and I found myself directly in front of that Federal major. The soldiers on either side of him were dead, but he was standing erect and blasting away with his revolver. This was the second time I had come face-to-face with an officer, and I knew what the outcome would be if I flinched, so I dropped the reins and filled both hands with guns.

I fired both pistols at once, and one shot caught him in the shoulder and the other shattered his kneecap. He dropped to the ground with a surprised look on his face, then he rolled and came up on one elbow. He brought his gun up, but I cocked my pistols and gave it to him again. Both of these rounds hit him in the middle of the chest, and he sprawled backward, his eyes open and staring up.

By the time I looked around to see where Frank was, it was over. All of Johnston's men were either dead or dying. Frank had returned to take the body of his friend from the field, and Little Archie Clement was on the ground with a knife pressed to the throat of a man who had a terrible chest wound that made a sucking sound when he breathed.

"Are there more of you?" Clement asked.

"Go to hell," the soldier wheezed.

"After you," Clement said as he slit his throat.

I dropped my reins, slid down from the saddle, and checked to see if my foe still lived. He did not. So I closed my eyes and took the gun from his warm hand.

Anderson rode over.

"Zeus's wounds," he roared as he reached down and snatched up the sword from where Johnston had planted it in the earth. "You've killed yourself a major, Dingus. Here, don't you want your prize?"

"You can have it," I said.

Clement had found another wounded soldier, this one just a boy. He held the gruesome knife to his throat and repeated the question. The soldier clenched his blood-stained teeth and remained silent.

"Your comrade was lung shot," Clement said in a voice that was almost a whisper. "They never survive. I did him a favor by sparing him the pain. But you, lad, are hardly touched—a round through the cheek and a busted leg, those are just scratches. Don't you want to live?"

The soldier licked his lips.

"That's it," Clement said. "Tell me what we need to know. How many like you are waiting for us?"

The soldier told about the rest of the infantry at Centralia, then pleaded to be taken back even as Clement was cutting him from ear to ear. Clement walked away as the boy clamped both of his hands around his throat in a futile attempt to stop the torrent of blood.

Anderson led us back to Centralia, where we killed most of the remaining infantry and chased the rest to the safety of a blockhouse. By the time we gave up, we had slain one hundred and fourteen of them.

Our casualties?

Three dead, a few others wounded.

13

The White Flag

BLOODY BILL GOT his headlines. About a month after the Centralia fight, he was shot dead during an ambush in Ray County.

We had stopped that morning at a farm, where Anderson had demanded breakfast, as usual. Anderson was feeling good, and as he waited to eat, he groomed himself and talked to his own reflection in a mirror. "Good morning, Captain Anderson. It's a pleasure to see you again. How are you today?" he asked himself. To this he replied, "Damn well, thank you." It had been one skirmish after another since our battle at Centralia, and although we knew the Federals were looking for revenge, we had no idea how close they actually were.

We left the farm about noon, with Anderson at the head of the column and about seventy of us strung out on the road behind. We had ridden only a short distance, when Anderson rounded a curve and was confronted by a line of infantryman blocking the road.

Anderson paused. The column sort of piled up around him, confused. Then Anderson reached for his pistols and gave a rebel yell as he charged, either not knowing or not caring how badly he was outgunned. Most of us followed, of course, but we were caught in the cross fire of at least a hundred guns. A dozen or so went down with that first volley, and the rest didn't want to stick around to see what a second would do. Those who still had horses beneath them slipped into the woods.

Anderson, however, survived the volley. They say he actually broke through the line before falling dead with two bullets in the back of his brain. The Yankees didn't even bother chasing the rest of us, because they had the object of their pursuit. Anderson's bridle of human scalps particularly fascinated them, as did his six revolvers and the hundreds of dollars in gold and bills that were found in his saddlebags.

The Yankees hauled Anderson's body to Richmond, Missouri, where they propped him up and took souvenir photos that sold for a nickel each. But the photos didn't do Bloody Bill justice, because they were taken a spell after he was shot, and his face had already swollen up. He looked like some kind of goon in the photos, but in life he was actually quite handsome. Finally, they cut off his head, stuck it on the end of a pole, and displayed it on the town square.

I'm not sure why they felt it was necessary to decapitate Bloody Bill after death. It was an unusual practice, even on the frontier, and it seemed like such a medieval thing to do. Were they afraid his spirit would come back to haunt them if they didn't separate his head from his body? That's how you kill monsters in fairy tales.

Clement tried to take command of what was left of Anderson's boys, but I finally stood up to the little bastard and said to hell with it. I cast my lot with David Pool, another of Anderson's lieutenants. Many of the others did too. We went to Texas for the winter, and in the spring we came back and fought wherever we could. But there was no organization or leadership to what we did, so we never represented much of a threat. Things just degenerated until we were forced to steal food to stay alive. Our glory days of looting whole towns and fighting the enemy toe to toe were gone.

Meanwhile, Quantrell had taken a few of his old comrades—including Frank—and had left the state. They were on a secret mission that Quantrell had cooked up to assassinate President Lincoln. Well, now you know that John Wilkes Booth had the idea first.

In May, Quantrell and the boys were ambushed on a farm in Kentucky by a group of rangers, which I guess is the Yankee equivalent of guerrilla. Quantrell slipped in the mud and horseshit of the barnyard while trying to mount his horse, and despite the efforts of Frank and some of the other men to help him, was shot in the spine. He spent about three weeks under guard at a Louisville hospital, paralyzed from the arms down, before he finally died.

Lee had surrendered during the second week of April 1865, but the news took more than a month to reach those of us in the bush. When it did, we wished it had taken even longer. We did not want to admit the war was over, we were afraid of what the Yankees would do to us if we surrendered, and it did not seem that we had much to return home to. But we could not remain in the bush.

At about the same time that Frank was trying to save himself and his captain in that muddy barnyard in Kentucky, me and forty other guerrillas rode into Lexington and negotiated our surrender. In exchange for not being hung, we surrendered our guns and grudgingly took the oath of loyalty. After a day or so I bid my comrades goodbye and pointed the nose of my horse toward Nebraska Territory. During the last year of the war, Mother and the rest of the family had abandoned the Clay County farm and sought the protection of relatives there.

I was crossing a stream some distance outside of town, when I heard the report of a single rifle shot and simultaneously felt myself being torn from my saddle and flung through the air. It felt as if the very fist of God had reached down from the heavens and smote me in the middle of the chest.

I landed on my back in the middle of the bridge, staring up at a dappled canopy of trees, unable to move or to draw breath for several seconds. I heard the bushes rustle a few yards down the road, then footsteps running in the opposite direction. When I did finally manage a breath, it was as if I were drawing fire into my chest instead of air, and that was when I recognized the horrible sucking sound.

I was lung shot.

And whoever had shot me did not explain why.

There must have been a hundred reasons to pick from, but I suppose the most likely motive was revenge for the Centralia massacre. The Lexington papers had announced that we forty had been part of Anderson's group. For a relative or a comrade or a friend of one of those poor naked soldiers that we had butchered, that would be enough—no need to ask names, any guerrilla will do. And I understood all this as I lay there across the wooden planks with a pool of my own blood growing around me. I understood the mechanics of revenge perfectly well.

I wasn't in pain, not at first, and my mind was incredibly sharp and time seemed to slow down. I reckoned the sniper was an infantryman, because the report of the rifle sounded characteristically like that of an Enfield. I would have preferred that my assassin walk over and introduce himself after the coup de grâce, or at least yell something that I could understand—*Roast in hell, secesh!* would have been appropriate—but I was not given that choice.

Instead, I heard the tops of trees stir, and then I felt a

great wind descend upon my body and kiss my cheek. The voice of God rang in my ears, and He said: "The arrows of death at noonday fly unseen." For the first time, I understood that passage to mean bullets—you can't see bullets in flight, can you? Invisible, they strike you down. And their arcs occupy such a brief instant of time that only God can mark their path.

Strangely, I was not panicked or afraid of dying. Instead, a quiet calm came over me. I had finally received the punishment I deserved, and whether I lived or died, that debt would be paid in full. For the first time in a long while, I prayed and did not try to barter with God over my fate.

"Thank you for my life," I whispered to myself. "It has been rough at times and is none too pleasant now, but you gave me a good home and a loving mother and brother that would follow me to hell and back. That's where I reckon I'm going now, and it's a one-way ticket, because I've never been baptized. But if it is your will that I survive, I will rectify that situation as soon as I'm on my feet. If not, please take care of my family."

My odds for survival were not good. I was lung shot, alone, and far outside town. My only chance was to summon help, but when I attempted to shout for help, I could force no sound from my blood-flecked lips. The pain was coming now, and it was like a fire that blazed in time to my beating heart. The mental sharpness I spoke of began quickly to fade.

My horse had returned, after first running for a short distance, and I looped one hand through a stirrup and tried to pull myself up. But she was skittish because of the blood smell, and backed away. I released the stirrup, because I could not stand to be dragged.

I attempted to stand, but could not, so I crawled to the edge of the bridge. The creek was only a few feet below, and I thought if only I could scoop up some water to relieve my growing thirst, it would give me a little strength—enough, perhaps, to sling myself over the saddle. So I reached far down with my hat but could not reach the water. My mind had become really dull at this point, and my vision was narrowing. I inched a little farther over the edge, reached down with my hat, and rolled off the bridge into the water.

The water was not deep, but my face went under, and it took me several moments before I could summon the strength to push myself up. Then I grasped the root of a willow tree and pulled myself a little ways onto the bank. I intended to rest there for only a minute or two, but soon I found myself unable to move at all.

My head was at an angle where I could see the bridge, and the water flowing beneath it, and on top of the water was a dark ribbon that was my blood. Things didn't hurt much as long as I remained perfectly still; the water was warm, and the mud beneath my shoulders was soft. This was the kind of stream that would have plenty of fish in it. I thought of how much I had loved to roam the woods as a child, and how peaceful I had found it, and what a pleasant place this was to die. As my eyelids fluttered, and the light of the sun went out, my very last thought was of how long it would take the atoms of my blood to find their way to the ocean.

A German farmer who spoke no English found me and stuffed my wounds with rags. Although I remember none of it, they tell me he threw me in the back of his wagon, turned it around, and drove like mad back into Lexington. He rattled up in front of the Virginia Hotel in a cloud of dust, and a doctor was fetched from the closest saloon. The doctor glanced at me as I lay unconscious and bloody on the wagon bed, pronounced me dead, and started to walk away, when the German grabbed him by the sleeve and wouldn't let go until the doctor actually placed his ear against my chest and listened for respiration.

"Good God, this lad is still alive," the doctor is said to have exclaimed in amazement.

They carried me into the hotel, placed me on a bed, and shot me full of morphine. Then the doctor cut away my clothes and, without so much as washing his hands first, probed my wounds with his fingers. The minié ball had entered my chest beneath the left nipple, shattered a rib, pierced my lung, came within an inch of my heart, and exited cleanly between my ribs in the back. For the next hour or so the doctor worked feverishly, cleaning away bits of bone and plugging the holes, front and back, with lint and wet bandages. When he was done, he said I'd die anyway.

Then he called for a pitcher and a bowl and washed my blood from his hands.

Meanwhile, the German had taken my horse to the livery next door and brought my saddlebags—unopened— to my room. He left without saying a word.

I woke the next day, surprised to find myself among the living. The pain in my chest was intolerable. Sitting beside my bed was Rafe Jones, one of the boys I had surrendered with, and he tore open a packet of white powder and poured it into a glass of water.

"The sawbones said for you to drink this when you woke up," Rafe said as he placed the glass in my hand.

"What is it?" I asked.

"Morphine."

I drank the milky liquid, then lay back on the bed.

"How come you're here?"

"We were drinking whiskey at the saloon and the hotel keeper sent for us, because he figured the way you looked, you had to be one of us bushwhackers. Said somebody needed to watch you until you were well enough to move."

"So I'm going to live?"

"Maybe," Rafe said. "If the fever don't get you."

"Where's my horse?"

"It's gone," Rafe said. "They say he was taken over to the livery, but nobody can find him now. Your saddle wallets are here though. The German that brought you in left them here."

"A Dutchman? Who was he?"

"Hell, I don't know. Didn't see him."

"Do I have any money left?"

"I dunno," Rafe said.

He reached for the bags, which were on the floor, and examined the contents. "Well, you got your Bible, and the pistol which you hid from the Federals, and rolled up in your hose is about sixty dollars in gold."

"Good," I said. It was hard to talk, and I had to rest a bit before I continued. "Rafe, I want you to send a telegram to my folks and ask them to come get me."

"Okay," Rafe said. "Where are they?"

"Centerville, in Clay County," I said. The morphine was making it hard to concentrate. "No, that's not right. They went to Nebraska Territory. What was the name of that town? Rollo, maybe."

"Rollo."

"No, that's not it," I said. "Something else."

"Damn, Dingus, I've got to know where to send this thing."

"Rulo," I said. "Rulo, Nebraska Territory. Ask them to come get me, Rafe. I don't want to die in this Yankee hotel."

•   •   •

In just a couple of days Rafe had loaded me on a steamboat and sent me up the Missouri to Kansas City. There,
the Mimms family met me with a wagon and took me
back to their boarding home outside town.

John Mimms had married my Aunt Mary, on my father's side, and they had a daughter which they named after my mother. Confused? Hell, I couldn't keep it all
straight half the time, and I was a blood relative. The
Mimms family and the Woodson family—where my middle name comes from—were related by both blood and
marriage, because there was an awful lot of hitching
done between first and second cousins. So, when you
throw in the Jameses and the Samuels, you can see that I
was related to a lot of folks scattered between St. Joseph
and Kansas City. Before the war we saw each other often,
and we all tended to think alike, so of course my uncle
John Mimms quickly agreed when my mother contacted
him and asked if they could receive me when the boat
docked in Kansas City, and care for me until our home
in Clay County was once again established.

It had felt kind of strange traveling by riverboat instead of attacking one, and I just wished I had been in
better health so that I could have enjoyed the ride. It was
a good time to travel too, because the weather was still
springlike and pleasant. But I was in such bad shape that
when they brought me out onto the deck, all I could do
was stare at the sky.

When they carried me down the plank at Kansas
City, I had spent every dollar I had. The doctor took a little, and the hotel took a little, and then there was the
medicine and the bandages, and I gave Rafe some to buy
drinks for him and the boys, and finally the steamboat
ticket. The only things remaining in my saddlebags were

the Bible and my Colt navy. But that was all right, because fate had worked it so I had enough to make it to the bosom of my family.

The boarding business was not all that good during the summer of 1865, so I had a second-floor room all to myself with a window looking out over the green rolling hills. They placed me in a big bed with an iron headboard, and for a while I could get no rest because of the steady stream of family and friends that came to wish me well. They also told me how proud they were that I had fought so hard for them, although that part made me uncomfortable.

My mother came to visit, and she looked just as I had remembered—big and stern. She was full of herself and her opinions, and she had some charms and salves that a yarb doctor had given her. But the trip had taken its toll on me. Before I left Lexington, the wound on my chest had begun to fill with yellow pus. The doctor had said it was a good sign, and that it was a by-product of the regeneration of tissue, but I wasn't so sure. It smelled awful and itched, and soon after that the fever set in.

Before my mother even told me that Frank had gotten home safely from Kentucky, or that they were planning on putting the farm in working order again, she drew a straight-backed chair up close and asked what had happened outside Lexington. Most of the Mimms family and several friends were in the room as well, and they all quieted down to listen.

"I got shot, Ma," I said. "You know that."

"No, honey," she said, and placed a hand on my brow. "I want to know who it was that shot you."

I took a painful breath, licked my lips, and asked for some water. I knew that Mother would never settle for the truth about what had happened, or what I thought at the time, because there wasn't anybody to hate in the story. But by the time I handed her back the glass, the story just started telling itself.

"We were riding into Lexington under a white flag, so to speak," I said. "Me and a few of the boys who had ridden with Anderson. We were going in to negotiate terms with the Federal commander there, because we'd be damned if we would surrender unconditionally."

"This flag," Zerelda asked. "It was a white flag, a flag of truce?"

"That's right, Mother," I said. "It was a big one, made from a bedsheet we had gotten at a sympathetic farmhouse the night before. I was up at the head of the column when we crossed this bridge, just a few miles outside town. All of a sudden the Federals opened up on us with their rifles. I dropped from my horse into the water, but I managed to pull my pistol from my belt and shoot one of the horses out from under the cowards as they fled."

The navy I had brought with me was resting on the nightstand, and at this point everybody just sort of stared at it with awe. Mother reached out, grasped the pistol, and placed it in her lap.

"Careful, Ma," I said. "It's loaded."

"Of course it is," she said. "But you or your friends never saw any of their faces? You never heard any names mentioned in town?"

"Nope," I said.

"Too bad," she said, "or we'd repay the debt. What happened next?"

"The boys who were with me didn't go after the cowards because they saw how badly I was hurt, and they wanted to get me right to a doctor. So they threw me over the saddle and rode me right into the middle of Lexington, where they put me up in the best hotel and went and got a doctor out of the saloon next door. He was drunk and didn't want to come, but my friends did some persuading, if you know what I mean."

There was a chuckle from the audience here.

"This doctor patched me up, then shot me full of morphine to ease the pain. I was out like a light for a couple of days, and when I came to I discovered that I had already signed the loyalty oath. The Federals had come in while I was drugged and made me sign my name to it, otherwise it never would have happened."

"My Lord," Zerelda said. "That just shows you what kind of people those Yankees are. Well, we already knew that, because they killed innocent people and burned their homes to the ground. That's what you and Frank were fightin' against."

"Sometimes," I said, "you gotta fight fire with fire."

"What do you mean?" she asked.

"Nothin', Ma," I said. "I'm really tired. Do you mind if I rest for a spell?"

She gave me another packet of the white powder, and I drifted off to sleep.

Mother left in a couple of days and the novelty of having a wounded veteran in the Mimms household wore off. The person who volunteered to assume my care on a daily basis was Zerelda Mimms. She looked nothing like her namesake, however. A small girl with fine features, she never weighed more than a hundred pounds. She was nineteen or twenty at the time.

She seemed to enjoy her work, and she often sat beside my bed to sing to me or read from the local newspaper. I felt kind of uncomfortable at first, having a female so near me all the time, even though it was a family member. The most awkward times was when she would change my dressings and bathe me, but she did it with infinite care, and never did her smile betray how awful my wound really was. I soon became used to the feel of her fingers on my skin, and looked forward to the daily ritual, and especially the nearness of her. I started calling her Zee so that I wouldn't think of my mother.

Each day, however, I grew worse. The fever seemed to be eating me alive. It took more and more of the morphine to take the edge from the pain, and then one day when Zee could not stand to see me in such pain, she mixed a double dose of the powder.

I went to sleep and would not wake up. When my breathing slowed to nothing and my brow became so hot that you could see the heat rising from it in waves, Zee became frantic. She was sure that I would die. They summoned another healer.

This old man was a power doctor. He had never gone to medical school, but he had spent a lifetime treating folks using home remedies and superstitions. When he examined me, he shook his head and told them I was on death's door, but that he would do what he could. He boiled out my wound with carbolic acid, then packed it with a concoction of spiderwebs and axle grease, with a little gunpowder thrown in for good measure. Then he took a rounded stone from a leather bag, said some prayers over it, and placed it firmly over the hole in my chest. Zee said the stone was about the size of a person's palm and was made from some porous material. The doctor called it a madstone, she said, and claimed it had been taken from the stomach of a man-eating grizzly bear out west. The purpose of the stone was to draw out the evil, the doctor said. The stone was left in for a couple of days, then the doctor removed it, had the Mimmses boil it, then slipped it back into its leather bag.

Then he ordered them to strip all the bedclothes away and burn them, and to keep only a light sheet over my naked body until I either recovered or died.

I was unconscious for three days and had the dream where I remembered being born, which I've already told you about. Zee never left my side until I woke up, which was in the cool of the morning just before dawn.

"Jesse?" Zee asked.

"Yes," I said. "I'm here."

Zee broke down and cried, she was so glad. She sat beside me on the bed, held my face in her hands, and smothered me with kisses. She lit a candle on the night-stand, then she got some warm water from the tank in the stove and some other supplies.

She began to wash my body so carefully and lovingly that it reminded me of something from the Bible. Maybe the one about Mary Magdalene bathing Jesus. Or perhaps I was thinking of one of the stories about the Round Table, the one where the wounded knight is nursed back to health by a beautiful princess. If I had a better education, I could probably tell you which story.

"You're going to be all right now, Jesse," she said as she washed my face. "Don't ask me how I know, but I just do. You are such a handsome boy, and people are going to know your name. The others don't know you like I do."

"What do you mean?" I asked.

She smiled as she placed my right hand in her lap.

"It doesn't matter to me what you've done," she said as she ran the sponge down my arm. "I don't care how many towns you've burned or what you've stolen. Or how many women you've had."

She held my right hand to her lips and kissed the fingers.

"How many men have you killed with this hand?" she asked.

I started to lie, to say that I hadn't counted.

"Seventeen," I said. "Ones that I know for sure anyway. Probably more, in the heat of battle."

"Did any of them look you in the eye?"

"Yes," I said.

She held the hand to her breast.

"I don't know why, Jesse," she said, "but that does excite me."

She dried my hand with a soft cloth. Then she repeated the operation with the other arm. She examined that hand by the light of the candle and asked me about the missing tip of the middle finger.

"Was it shot away?" she asked.

"No," I said. "I did it myself while fiddling with my revolver. It was foolish."

She kissed the fingers of that hand.

"Have you had many women?" she asked.

"Not many," I said. "There wasn't really the chance in the bush, except for the crib girls when we came to a town of any size, and they never interested me. We left the good women, the clean women—like you, Zee—we left them alone, mostly. Some of the boys got a little rough at times, but I never saw them take advantage."

She nodded.

"No one else?"

"No," I lied.

Then she folded down the sheet and began to wash my chest, being careful not to disturb the bandages. She paused at the little puckered spot where I had been shot the first time.

"I've wondered about this," she said.

"A pistol ball did that," I said. "The ball's still in there too, lodged in a rib."

She kissed the spot, then turned her attention to my stomach. The sponge sliding up and down my skin felt so good that my eyes threatened to roll to the back of my head. Then I felt a familiar tug in the bottom of my belly, a sort of electric twitch, and then the warm rush of blood to my dingus.

"Don't," I said, and moved her hand away.

"Don't you like me?" she asked. She sounded disappointed.

"Of course I do," I said. "But what if your father comes in?"

"Don't worry about him," Zee said. "He's afraid of you. Do you know that? All the men are."

"Are you afraid of me?" I asked.

"No," she said, and pulled the sheet all the way down. "Will you marry me, Jesse?"

"Someday," said I.

14

Robbery Under Arms

O UR LOVE AFFAIR was no secret, and everyone just assumed Zee and I were engaged after that summer, although we made no formal announcement. Also, we never discussed a date for the wedding. Things were so dismal after the war, it seemed that we would never be in a position to start a family.

Thanks to Zee, my condition steadily improved. Within a few months I was able to return to the farm, where both Frank and I attempted to rebuild our lives. But times were rough, and there wasn't any money to buy the things we needed. Even if we had the money, it was unlikely that anybody would sell us land or cattle. The militia was now in unchallenged control of the state, and we chafed under the heel of the Yankee boot.

Because of the carpetbaggers, things were even tougher in some ways than during the war. They controlled the banks, the railroads, and the government. They passed a new state constitution that said there would be no amnesty for former rebels. We could not vote, hold public office, attend college, be a deacon of a church, or practice any of the principal professions. Also, I was personally indicted by a grand jury for killing that infantry major at Centralia.

Frank considered that ironic, because Johnston had been killed in one of our clearest stand-up fights. Still, Anderson had left his bloody stain across every page connected with the Centralia fight, and folks were looking for revenge. But it's one thing to charge somebody with a crime, and quite another to find somebody willing to bring him to trial—especially if the defendant is an ex-guerrilla. Nobody ever showed up to serve that warrant, but the thought of it troubled my sleep, and for many months I avoided going to town.

The only public appearance I made was at Mt. Gilead Baptist Church at Centerville, where I was dunked in a tank of water and baptized. I still had not fully recovered, but I reckoned it was time to make good on that promise.

It also inspired me to try for a peaceful life, at least for a spell. Frank and I gave honest labor our best shot, but the odds seemed so stacked against us that we always came away discouraged.

The memories of how easy it had been to take what we needed haunted us. How many thousands of dollars had passed through our hands when we were with Quantrell and Anderson? We should have buried some of it, but the thought never occurred to us that the South would really lose.

Along about February of 1866 I was feeling particularly discouraged. It had been a harsh winter, there was snow on the ground, and it didn't seem like we would ever be able to put things at the farm in order. I still had not healed, and could work only part of a day. My visits to Zee had become less and less frequent, because I couldn't bear to admit to her that my chances of ever supporting a family were growing dim.

One morning after breakfast I stepped out onto the wooden porch and asked Frank to join me. A few stars were still shining faintly in the west, and the fields were blanketed with snow. The trees were cased in ice, and icicles fringed the eaves of the cabin.

"Pretty out here," Frank said. He was leaning against a post and holding a steaming cup of coffee in his hand. "God, I do love this land. I only wish we could make a living. You know, we're about to starve to death."

"That's what I want to chat with you about," I said.

"Why out here?" he asked.

"Because I didn't want Ma and the others to hear."

Frank raised his eyebrows.

"Buck," I said, "it seems to me if the Yankees are going to keep treating us like the war never ended, we ought to return the favor."

He sipped his coffee.

"They won," he said.

"They're pissing on us," I said. "Everybody from the Jayhawkers to the goddamned state militia did the things we did, and worse, but we're considered criminals. Hell, your friend Bud Younger is so afraid he's going to be lynched that he won't even tell people his real name."

"I thought you were going to quit cussing," Buck said.

"I'm working on it," I said. "I may be a Christian now, but I'm still a man. Do you think the Founding Fathers ever intended for Americans to be treated this way? Buck, we have fewer rights than a stick of wood."

"Lumber never did have any rights."

"You know what I mean," I said.

"So what do you want to do about it?" Frank asked.

"I want our share, that's all."

"Let's go to the territories."

"No," I said. "This is our home."

"Then what?"

"We both remember how easy it was to take an entire town with just a handful of men who mean business.

Nobody would stand up to us because they didn't have the guts. We can do it again."

"You want to burn a town?"

"No," I said. "We just want their money. We can rob a bank."

"A bank?" Frank asked.

"Why not?"

"Because nobody's ever done it, at least not during peacetime," he said. "There are unwritten rules against it. You do that sort of thing only when you're at war."

"We're still at war."

Frank whistled.

"You're crazy, Dingus," he said.

"Of course I am. Anybody would be driven crazy in this situation, and the only thing that is going to get us out of it is money. The goddamned Yankee banks have all of our money locked up in their vaults. Do you think one penny of those loyalty bonds our people posted for stock and property was ever returned? We'll just take back our share."

"Like Robin Hood," Frank said, and smiled.

"Yes, dammit."

"You signed an oath of loyalty," he said.

"So did you. Did you mean it?"

"No."

"I was delirious," I said. "Neither did I."

"So we rob this bank," he said, warming to the idea. "Just the two of us?"

"No, we'll need a dozen or so. You remember the routine."

"They'll talk," Frank said.

"Would your friend Bud Younger talk?" I asked. "Now, think about it. Say we rob that bank over in Liberty. All of us get away except Bud. They haul him to jail and tell him they won't hang him as long as he identifies the others involved. Would he talk?"

"No."

"Would you talk?"

"No."

"And neither would any of the boys," I said.

"Liberty?" Frank asked.

"Liberty," I said. "It's far enough away that we won't be recognized, the bank is unprotected, and the weather will provide us cover. Besides, those Yankee bastards mocked us during the war."

Coleman Younger was a big lad with hands like mallets, and a pumpkin for a head. His face had kind of a raw and unshapen quality that made you think that perhaps God wasn't finished with him yet. Whenever he walked into a room, even if he was alone, it always seemed crowded. The difference in size was so great between us that the first time I met him I felt like a child being introduced to a grown-up.

But he had an easy, friendly quality about him, and never once did I see him use his size to bully anybody. He never raised his voice—well, at his size he never had to— and when he spoke, it was always after deliberating upon his words. When Frank and I outlined our plan to rob the Liberty bank, he listened carefully and said that we could count on him.

On the afternoon of February 13, 1866, we rode into Liberty with eleven other ex-rebels. There is no need to reveal their identities here. But I can report that they all agreed the town was a good choice, as a symbol if nothing else. Two years earlier, during the summer of 1864, the town had convened a public meeting and officially condemned us guerrillas as "monsters of society."

Our expectations were uncertain, and we had no guide except our wartime experience. It really did not occur to us that we were about to make history.

Newspaper accounts said we were all dressed in pieces of Federal uniforms to fool people that we were militia, but that is not so. I refused, as usual, to wear the Union blue, but most of the others wore Union pants or jackets as a practical matter. It was bitterly cold that day, and the boys simply piled on every scrap of clothing they owned. Both Cole and Frank wore officers' overcoats they had captured.

When we reached the town square, most of our boys took strategic positions around the bank, trying their best to act nonchalant and appear like they belonged there. But they needn't have worried. It was so cold that few people were out and nobody cared about a group of strangers, even if they were heavily armed young men in ragged clothes.

Most of the snow that had fallen earlier had melted by then. The streets had turned to mud for a couple of days when the sun was out and the temperature was above freezing, but overnight they had frozen hard again. The sky, however, looked like we were in for another snow that afternoon.

"Buck, I hate this weather," I said.

"Makes you stiff," he said.

"Hurts my eyes," I said as I rubbed them with the back of my hand.

"Don't do that," Frank said.

"I miss Texas," I said. "Do you like Texas? Why don't we go back there after we get Mother and the farm squared away. It's warm in Texas."

"But our home is Missouri," he said.

"Missouri," I spat out. "Misery is more like it. The only worse place I can imagine is Kansas."

"Kansas," Frank said, "is where you go after you die. But only if you've been bad."

The Clay County Savings Bank was located in a brick

building on the corner. It was clearly marked and had a large doorway and two windows that faced the street.

Frank and Cole dismounted and looped their reins around a post out front while I pretended to cinch my saddle nearby. Because of my weakened condition, I had promised Frank that I would wait outside.

They paused for a moment at the entrance, wiped their boots, and surveyed the street to make sure it was still deserted. Then they entered, and I watched what happened next through the windows.

The bank was empty except for a couple of employees working at their desks, a father and son team named William and Greenup Bird. I don't know what kind of name Greenup is, maybe the newspapers got it wrong, but it stuck in my mind.

Frank warmed his hands over a stove while Cole went to the counter and asked, as we had planned, to change a note. Greenup, the cashier, was on the other side of the counter, and I saw him ask something, it must have been what denomination or series or something. Cole reached inside his coat as if to produce the bill, but instead came out with a revolver cocked and pointed at Greenup's chest.

Then Cole said they were both dead men if they didn't give them all the money they had.

At this point the younger Bird objected.

Frank jumped over the counter, grabbed William Bird by the collar, and beat him about the ears with the butt of his gun. Then Frank forced him into the vault, produced a grain sack from a pocket of his coat, and ordered the bleeding man to fill it with coins.

Meanwhile, Cole was holding his pistol on the elder Bird with one hand and searching the teller's drawer with the other. He dumped the change box and started scooping bonds and greenbacks from the bottom of the drawer.

Then Cole shoved the old Bird into the vault with the young one, and Frank swung the door shut.

When they emerged from the bank, their hands were so full, it looked like a cartoon of a bank robbery. In addition to the grain sacks that held notes, bonds, and coins, there were three more sacks of silver and gold that had been entrusted to the bank for safekeeping.

Then the fools in the bank started yelling their heads off about being robbed. Their cries were muffled at first, but then they pushed on the vault door and discovered that Frank hadn't locked it, so they ran to the window directly in front of me and started screaming and pointing.

Frank and Cole were not yet on their horses.

I produced my pistol and pointed it at the Birds, who both ducked beneath the safety of the sill. But it was too late; their cries had already gotten the attention of two men on the sidewalk opposite the bank. I cursed our luck, because for ten minutes the street had been clear in both directions.

The two men stopped, and their faces turned and I knew they saw Frank and Cole with the loot. The men were so bundled in clothes that I could not tell if they were old or young, or whether they were armed.

"Stay where you are," I shouted, and sent a round over their heads for good measure.

They stopped for a moment, then one of them took a step in my direction. His face was half covered by a muffler, and he had something in his right hand, something that looked an awful lot like a gun.

Instinctively, I fired.

The man stumbled and went down at the edge of the street.

Some of our boys threw a few rounds at his buddy, and one of them fluffed the pocket of his jacket for him. He ran for the nearest house.

Frank and Cole were mounted now, and they yelled for me to follow. I swung up into the saddle, and then I allowed myself a good look at the man I had just killed.

He was on his back with his arms flung out and the soles of his boots pointed at me. A pool of his blood was seeking the gutter. The blood steamed in the cold, just as if somebody had thrown a pot of hot coffee into the street. Not far from his outstretched left hand was a book. The book was open and its pages were rustling in the winter wind.

A book.

He had been carrying a book.

How could I have mistaken it for a gun?

Frank rode back and tugged at my sleeve.

"Come on, Jesse," he yelled. "Don't worry about him. He's dead. You said this was a war, right? Well, people die in wars."

"Yeah, but—"

Frank fired his pistol into the ground, and my horse bolted.

As we thundered out of Liberty, with the boys whooping and hollering, it began to snow. Our tracks would be covered. According to plan, we split up into two groups at the Missouri River. One went north, the other went south, and we even recrossed the river a couple of times for good measure. Later that night, in the midst of a snowstorm, we gathered at the Mt. Gilead Baptist Church to divide the loot.

When we counted the money, none of us could quite believe our luck. There was sixty thousand dollars in the notes and bonds, and another twenty thousand in metal. And in those days, eighty thousand dollars was quite a bit more money than it seems now.

It was, quite simply, a small fortune.

Some of the boys were leery of the bonds, but Cole

Younger volunteered to cash them and distribute the proceeds. Frank and Cole got extra shares because they had taken the most risk, as did I for coming up with the idea. The rest of the money was divided evenly among the rest, and when we left the cold church and ventured back into the night, each of us was rich—at least by Missouri standards. I wanted to leave a little something on the altar behind us, but the others said no, somebody would just steal it.

The newspapers reported the robbery with vigor.

Never before had there been a daylight bank robbery during peacetime, they said. A seven-thousand-dollar reward was posted by the sheriff and the bankers at Liberty. Folks were pretty certain that a group of former guerrillas had robbed the bank, but they didn't have names or faces to go with the theory. Three former rebels were arrested on general principle and thrown in jail but were eventually released. None of the three had taken part.

And the bystander I had killed?

His name was George Wymore, but his friends and family called him Jolly. He was a student at William Jewell College at Liberty. He was going to be a preacher. The spooky thing is that my father had helped found that college.

15

Practice Makes Perfect

THEY SAY MONEY can't buy you happiness, but
poverty is no substitute either, as our mother has
always been quick to point out. Our share of the
Liberty loot seemed like such a powerful lot of money
that Frank and I never thought we'd have to do it again,
and we *were* happy for a while. We were able to put food
on the table, buy some stock, and put the farm in order.
Then I wrote the Wymore boy's parents a long letter
telling them how sorry I was, and that it had been an accident, of course, and how I would give anything in the
world to take back that one moment when I saw a gun in
the kid's hand instead of a book. I mailed it too. But of
course I couldn't sign it.

Then Frank got kind of nervous because it got back
to him that somebody thought they had recognized him
at Liberty, although they weren't sure. So Frank left to
visit our uncle in Kentucky until things cooled off a little,
and I'll be damned if he didn't get into a scrap with four
drunken troopers down there and end up killing two of
them and getting shot in the hip himself.

Frank beat it to the home of our uncle, George Hite,
and then he sent for me. So I packed up and made the
trip down there, and we spent the next few months

recuperating together, and to tell the truth, it was kind of pleasant to be able to spend some of the money on ourselves and not worry about attracting too much attention.

But traveling is expensive and the money did not last as long as we had expected. In eight months we were back in Missouri and plotting our next robbery. After all, the first had seemed so easy and rewarding enough.

Our target was the Mitchell and Company banking house at Lexington. Cole Younger, my brother Frank, and I were the principals, and would be backed up by a half dozen of our former saddle mates.

On the afternoon of October 30, 1866, Frank and Cole entered the bank and asked the cashier to change a one-hundred-dollar note. The cashier refused, claiming they were not presently in need of such funds, but the truth was the strangers made him nervous. Then I entered the bank, pointed my pistol at the cashier, and said: "We'll kill you if you don't give us one hundred thousand dollars."

The cashier laughed.

"What's so funny?" I asked.

"You are," the cashier said. "We don't have those kinds of funds on hand."

Beginner's luck had ruined us. We reckoned that stating up front our demands, and attempting to increase our total take by twenty percent, was entirely reasonable. We were ignorant of the ways in which assets changed, like the seasons, and thought all banks at all times were miniature treasure houses.

But I was pigheaded and did not believe the fellow, so I demanded the key to the vault. He said he didn't have it, I threatened to kill him, and then he pointed out that killing him wouldn't produce the key. In the end we were forced to take what we could find in the drawers, which was a little under two thousand.

When we split the loot, it hardly seemed worth the effort.

"Dammit, Frank," Cole raged after we were far enough away to converse without looking over our shoulders. "Jesse just doesn't have the experience to lead this gang. Our lives are forfeit if we let him do all the planning."

"Don't ask me to choose between you and Jesse," Frank said. "You're my best friend, but he's my brother, and you know what they say about blood being thicker than water. Besides, robbing banks was his idea."

"But I've got the experience," Cole fumed.

"I know," Frank sighed. "You were one of Charley Quantrell's captains. But Jesse acquitted himself right well with Anderson, and I was no slouch either."

"But—"

"The leader is the one with the best plan," Frank said. "When you have a better plan than Jesse, you let us know. We're on the same side here, Bud."

"Yeah," Cole said, "but to me he'll always just be your kid brother."

So, after having invented bank robbery, we were now faced with the challenge of perfecting it. Others were horning in on the act too, but that's how things go with a good idea. And things were not always as friendly within our own gang as they might have been. Often I suspected that Cole may have been doing some moonlighting, but I never had any proof.

We got better with practice and soon were pulling jobs on the average of once every six or eight months, which is generally how long the money lasted. In between jobs we would travel. I went to New York, once, but found it uncomfortable. Frank and I then went to California, by way of Panama, and tried to find our father's grave at Hangtown, with no luck. But our uncle Drury owned a hotel and mineral spa at Paso Robles, and we spent many pleasant days there—as long as the money held out.

At first we made withdrawals only from banks in Missouri and Kentucky, but later we also visited Iowa, Kansas, Arkansas, and Texas. I can't really count Minnesota, but we'll get to that presently.

Nobody agrees now on how many banks we actually did rob. I reckon the total must have been around twenty-five, but the thing of it is, we robbed so many banks during our career—and later, stagecoaches, trains, and even the Kansas City Fairgrounds once—that it's hard for me to remember them all. We even *wrecked* a train once, although we meant only to stop it. It amuses me to read books arguing that I couldn't have been at this or that robbery because I was ailing from my chest wound, or was suffering from a head cold that day, or because the style of the bandits was so ungentlemanly that it couldn't possibly have been me or my gang.

In a way, all the good robberies—the ones that went according to plan—felt like one long robbery to me, because the same things happened. We would walk in, ask to change a bill, joke about the discount the bank would give us, and then when the cashier balked we would pull our guns and rob the hell out of them.

The first five years after we started were the best, because we were hitting towns that we had become acquainted with during the war, our friends hid us, and the authorities had not identified us. Not only did the law not know our names, they didn't even have a decent description of us. None of the witnesses could agree on what we looked like. No warrants, no wanted posters, and, especially—no Pinkertons.

16

Bad Citizens

I NEVER HAD the pleasure of meeting Allan Pinkerton
in person, and you can be certain that if I had, the
pleasure would indeed have been mine and not his,
for I would have shot the sonuvabitch dead.

Pinkerton, you see, was the founder of the Chicago
detective agency whose symbol is the eye that never
sleeps. Just as my brother and I had invented modern
bank robbery, Pinkerton had invented the modern idea of
the "private eye."

But beyond being natural enemies, Pinkerton waged
a personal war against us that brought more misery to my
family than any other individual. He and his Yankee organization would eventually stoop to hellish lows in their
efforts to capture us, as you shall see, but at first they
were merely an annoyance.

Pinkerton was born in Scotland but came to America
as a boy, and while working as a cooper he stumbled upon
a counterfeiting ring and was responsible for their capture. He apparently found the experience so thrilling that
he immediately decided to become a detective, and after
a few false starts found himself working for the railroads.

He was still working for the railroads when he chanced
upon a plot to assassinate President Lincoln and foiled

it, then was elevated to a member of General George
McClellan's staff. His absurd estimates of Confederate
troop strength—some four or five times the actual
number—paralyzed an already cautious McClellan, and
inadvertently contributed to a string of Southern vic-
tories in the early years of the war.

Pinkerton's interests were always connected with the
railroads in some fashion or other, and it was railroad
business that brought the James Gang to his attention.
But I guess we sort of invited it.

Around the first week of June of 1871 we swung up
to Corydon, Iowa, and robbed the Ocobock Brothers'
Bank while most of the town was at the Methodist
Church to listen to an address by Henry Dean Clay. The
famous antislavery speaker was in town urging support
for a new railroad, and that's where the Pinkerton connection came in.

It was one of the easier jobs we had pulled, because
the cashier was alone in the bank, and we rode away with
ten thousand dollars without having to fire a shot in
anger. But as we were passing the Methodist church on
our way out of town, I couldn't resist paying a visit.

The four of us—Cole, Frank, myself, and a new man by
the name of Clell Miller—walked into the packed church
while Clay was droning on about economic prosperity.

"Pardon me," I said.

Our guns were hidden under our dusters, so we didn't
frighten anyone. A woman near me told me to hush up.
Couldn't I see that the great man was still speaking?

"Well, yes," I said. "But I just thought you good
folks would want to know that your bank has just been
robbed."

"That's ridiculous," a man called.

"Shame on you for trying to disrupt this meeting,"

another shouted. "You're just another bunch of farm boys who are mad at the railroads."

"No, sir," I said. "Your bank has just been robbed, and we're just trying to do the neighborly thing by letting you know. But seeing as how you don't care—"

"We think you'd better leave," somebody said.

"All right," I said, backing down the aisle. "But tomorrow morning, don't say I didn't warn you. Sorry to interrupt, Dr. Clay, but we have business elsewhere. Good day."

Later, when they discovered the cashier tied up and their money gone, the notion that we somehow represented an anti-railroad faction stuck. Allan Pinkerton, of the Pinkerton Detective Agency in Chicago, must have read about it in the newspapers, because he sent one of his sons to investigate.

The Pinkertons tracked us back to Missouri and arrested Clell Miller for taking part in the robbery. Now, once they got to Missouri it did not take a great deal of detective work to hear the names of the James boys and Cole Younger in the same sentence as "bank robbery." But they knew Clell Miller was a recent saddle buddy of ours and arrested him instead. I think they figured that Clell was our weakest link, and was most likely to testify about who was there in order to save his own neck.

That was just Clell's luck for you—his first bank job, and he gets thrown in jail. He had about the same luck during the war, when as a fourteen-year-old he joined Anderson just three days before Bloody Bill was killed. Clell was one of the few that were captured at the ambush, and he spent the rest of the war at the Jefferson Barracks at St. Louis.

When they found out that Clell wouldn't talk, the Pinkertons starting feeding the newspapers stories about how they suspected some members of the James and Younger families were involved in the robbery. They were obviously hoping for our Missouri neighbors to betray us. But they had miscalculated how well us ex-rebels would stick together.

Clell was tried in Iowa, but some of our friends made the trip up there to testify that he had been with them on the day of the bank robbery, so he was acquitted.

After that we were never free of the detectives.

Folks began talking about the "James Gang," as we were now being called, because of what they read in the newspapers. I started writing letters to the newspapers in our defense, claiming that Frank and I had been unjustly accused of crimes we did not commit, and a mountain of other horseshit, just like Bloody Bill used to.

After we robbed the cash box of a thousand dollars at the Kansas City Exposition in the fall of 1872, the newspapers were full of their usual speculations about whether the James Gang was involved. This may have been partly my fault, because I proudly announced to the cashier that he was getting robbed by "one Jesse James" when I demanded the money. The robbery had gone pretty well, at least until that damned cashier who was in charge of the box tried to wrest it back, and a shot was fired that struck the leg of a little girl standing in line with her mother. My brother fired that shot, and he felt terrible bad about it later, and was glad when we learned that the little girl was going to be all right. Cole and I cussed him for it, but it wouldn't be the last time that Buck would fire a parting shot the rest of us would regret. There was something wrong with him in that way—in person he was the most sensible and measured man I knew, full of book learning and compassion, but when he got behind a gun, he seemed to be transported body and soul back to the war, and the odds were good that somebody would get hurt. Most of the newspapers deplored the crime, as would anyone when discussing a crime during which a child was seriously hurt, but the *Kansas City Times* published a curious piece that made us out to be heroes—and not just any heroes, mind you, but the greatest heroes of all time. It was written by the editor of the newspaper, a man by the name of Major John Newman Edwards, who had fought with Shelby during the war. He had even followed Shelby and the Iron Brigade when it crossed the Rio Grande, dropped the Stars and Bars in the water, and offered their services to Maximilian.

"These men are bad citizens," Edwards said of us, "but they are bad because they live out of their time. The nineteenth century with its sybaritic civilization is not the social soil for men who might have sat with Arthur at the Round Table, ridden at tourney with Sir Lancelot, or won the colors of Guinevere."

He also said we were robbers of such a caliber that if we met the legendary robbers Dick Turpin or Claude Duval, we probably would have taken loot from them. And, Edwards said, although it was despicable, the robbery was "a deed so high-handed, so diabolically daring, and so utterly in contempt of fear that we are bound to admire it and revere its perpetrators."

The article, as well as ones in surrounding papers, reported that Frank and I were known to be in the vicinity at the time of the robbery.

Well, what can you say to something like that?

"I have just read your article charging Frank and myself with robbing the ticket office at the exposition grounds," I shot back in a letter. "This charge is baseless and without foundation, and as you have always published all articles that I have sent you, I will write just a few lines on the subject.

"I can prove where I was at the very hour the gate was

robbed, and have several upstanding citizens who will be glad to testify that I was miles away from Kansas City. But rest assured that I will not allow myself to be arrested on this false charge, because a man charged with robbery these days is most invariably set upon by a mob after he is captured, and hung or murdered without judge or jury. If I could have a fair trial I would prove my innocence before any jury in the state, but a fair trial is impossible for sons of the South. Also, I'd like to point out that neither Cole Younger nor his brother John participated in the robbery, and the people who said they saw us on the road together outside Kansas City that day are bald-faced liars. If the civil authorities have anything to communicate to us, let them answer through the *Times*."

I thought it was a fine piece of Missouri journalism, but Cole was madder than King George when he read it. He came tearing up to the farm with the newspaper beneath his arm, and he dragged me by my elbow outside to the yard. My brother Frank was out in the fields that day, and Cole and I were alone, which always was an uncomfortable proposition.

"Jesse," he said, "I have underestimated you, for you are a bigger fool than even I had believed. How dare you take it upon yourself to defend the Youngers in your letter?"

"Why, I thought I was doing you a turn."

"Nobody suspected my brother John," Cole roared, and beat me over the head with the folded newspaper. "You are the dumbest sonuvabitch that ever put his butt in a saddle. If you ever do anything like this again, Dingus, I'm going to thrash you."

I snatched the newspaper away from him.

"Don't call me Dingus," I said. "Only my brother can call me that."

"Dingus, Dingus, Dingus," Cole said. "And don't go getting that mad-dog look in your eye. Get your hand off your iron. Frank is not here to defend you, and I will kill you dead if you even act like you're going to pull a pistol on me."

Cole sent a letter to the Pleasant Hill paper, where all his old friends in Cass County could read it.

"My name would never have been used in connection with the affair had not Jesse W. James for some cause best known to himself published in the *Kansas City Times* a letter stating that John, he, and myself were accused of the robbery. Let me state here, once and for all, that no Youngers were involved in the robbery of the Kansas City Exposition. We were in the Kansas City area visiting our sisters at the time, and would never have considered participating in such an ill-conceived plan."

From that time on, the papers began to refer to us as the "James-Younger Gang," and I don't know if that irked Cole or me the most. It was always simply supposed to be the James Gang, period, and the Youngers were helpers.

But with our names on every tongue, the Pinkertons felt more and more pressure to do something about us. Things heated up for the next couple of years and then boiled over in 1874.

The Pinkertons hired a young undercover detective by the name of James W. Whicher to infiltrate our gang, and the fool got off the train in Liberty and started asking directions to the James-Samuel farm. He let it be known that he was a rough desperado, and that his ambition was to join the James boys in some daring robberies. The sheriff and others told him that the plan would never work, but he was intent on "arresting us in our own homes." He was last reported seen outside Kearney—which is what they started calling Centerville now—at 5:45 P.M. on March 10, walking toward our place.

He got to our place after dark. He told us his name was Allen, and claimed to be a drifter looking for work.

We let him in and fed him some supper, but everything about him just didn't seem right. He was too clean for one thing, and although his clothes were dirty, they did not have that well-worn look of somebody who has been on the road. He also spoke too well, without a trace of a backwards Missouri twang, and seemed to know little about the war. Then, when he announced his intention of joining the James Gang, we were sure he was some kind of authority.

"Pardon my boldness," he said, "but I reckon men like you are looking for boldness. If you could use an extra hand, I would be honored."

His hands were shaking. We were all sitting around the big table in the kitchen, and when he had finished delivering his speech, Frank pushed his plate away.

"Mother," he said, "I'm not hungry now. Would you please excuse Jesse and me, because you know how we hate to discuss business at the table."

Perry Samuel, the twelve-year-old black boy who had taken to helping Aunt Charlotte run things, took up Frank's plate and put it on the stove to warm. I motioned for him to take mine as well.

John Thomas Samuel, our thirteen-year-old half brother, and little Archie Peyton Samuel, who was just eight, protested that they were not yet done. Pappy just looked distracted and kept stabbing at his mashed potatoes.

"No trouble in the house, boys," Mother said quietly.

"Come on," I said. "Let them finish. We'll step out onto the porch."

Once outside, Frank lit a cigar for himself. Then offered this man called Allen one. Nervously, he took it.

"What about Jesse?" Allen asked. "Doesn't he want a cigar?"

"Jesse doesn't smoke," Frank said. "It irritates his lung condition."

"Beautiful out here, ain't it?" I asked.

"Yes, sir," Allen said enthusiastically.

"Right here is where I first suggested to Buck that we rob the Liberty bank," I said. "And now you're here. Do you know what that means?"

"I think so," he said. "I'm honored to be one of your gang."

"Did you enjoy supper?" Frank asked.

"I'm beholden to you," he said. "The cigar is fine, and so was the dinner. The fried chicken was the best I've had in a long while. Being on the road and all."

"That's good," Frank said, and nodded. "Because it's the last you'll ever have."

I produced my pistol from inside my coat while Frank began to search him.

"You've got this all wrong," Allen sputtered.

"We don't think so," Frank said as he took a .32-caliber revolver from the top of Allen's boot. "You must be a Pinkerton man, because you tend to favor tiny little guns you can hide. Where's your badge?"

"I'm not a Pinkerton, I swear it."

Frank turned the gun over. On the frame was stamped P.G.G., which stood for Pinkerton Government Guard.

"What were you going to do, shoot us while we slept?" I asked.

"I bought that pistol used," he stammered.

"You're not even a convincing liar," I said.

"You make a sorry undercover agent," Frank added.

He hung his head.

"I'm sorry," he said. "Let me free and I'll go back to Chicago and tell Mr. Pinkerton that he's wasting his time sending men after the James boys."

"I wish we could," Frank said. "But the moment you stepped into this house you were a dead man."

"Why's that?" the condemned man managed to say through dry lips.

"Because none of you fellows has ever gotten a good look at us. Not one of your descriptions has been worth two cents. But now you've seen me and Jesse up close for about an hour, and have seen the inside of our house, and have talked to our family. We're sorry, but this is a deadly game, and you have lost."

Then I hit him on the top of the head with the butt of my revolver, and he fell like a load of bricks. I felt sorry for him too, because he was about my age. But he obviously had more guts than brains.

We found the badge in the hollowed-out heel of his boot.

We tied him up and gagged him and threw him across a horse. By the time it took him across the Blue River by ferry at three o'clock in the morning, he was awake and squirming. Frank and I told the ferrymen that the captured man was a horse thief, and that we were officers, and needed to look for his accomplice on the other side of the river.

They found him the next day, outside Independence, still trussed up. Frank had put a bullet in his brain while I placed one in his heart. Then we threw the badge on top of him.

At about the same time that this Pinkerton agent named Whicher visited us in Clay County, more detectives were seeking the Youngers in St. Clair. The Youngers had abandoned their burned-out home in Cass County and moved to the middle of the state after the war.

Two Pinkertons by the name of Louis Lull and James Wright attended a dance at the Monagaw Hotel on March 16. The Youngers were frequent visitors to the mineral springs resort, which was situated at the base of an impressive cliff that overlooked half the county, but they were not in attendance that night.

The next day, the two Pinkertons were in the company of local constable Ed Daniels, when they were overtaken by a couple of riders on the road outside the little town of Roscoe. The riders were John and Jim Younger, and they knew the strangers had been asking too many questions about their family.

The Pinkerton named Wright took off when he saw the Youngers approach, but Lull and Daniels held their ground. After a brief and unpleasant interrogation, Lull drew a small Smith & Wesson and shot John Younger through the neck. John then hit Lull in the shoulder with a load of buckshot. When the constable bolted, Jim Younger shot him dead.

Lull tried to escape through the woods, but John—who was suffering badly from his neck wound—gave chase. When Lull was knocked from his horse by a low branch, John shot him in the chest with the shotgun. But before John Younger could ride back to his brother, he fell dead from his horse.

Cole Younger, who was in Hot Springs, Arkansas, at the time of the Roscoe gun battle, read about the death of his twenty-four-year-old brother in the newspaper.

17

Family Business

THE SCORE WAS three dead Pinkertons and one dead Younger.

But you have to put John Younger in a category all by himself, because he had never been one of our gang. So afraid were his brothers that the detectives would dig up John's body that they buried him at night in an unmarked grave in a country cemetery not far from the shootout, but angled his head to the northeast so they would be able to find it in the years to come.

The Pinkertons publicly accused the good folks of Clay County of harboring outlaws, and abetting in the death of that fool Whicher. Silas Woodson, the governor of the state of Missouri, persuaded the state legislature to fund an organization of secret agents to fight the outlaws.

But neither the Pinkertons nor any other authority beyond the borders of Clay County had any idea what we looked like. There were no photographs, at least not outside the family, and the descriptions of eyewitnesses were so vague as to fit half the male population.

We traveled about in Clay County just as freely as we always had, and when we traveled, it was convenient to adopt an alias. I tended to favor names that had some connection to our extended family—Woodson, or Thoma-son, or Howard.

If anybody asked our business, we'd just tell them we were stock buyers up from Texas. The story was believ-able because we looked like stock buyers, with our linen dusters over our fine suits, and we were always ready to buy fine horses, and Cole Younger often invested in cat-tle. Our guns didn't arouse much attention either, be-cause nobody traveled unarmed from state to state in those days, leastways not on horseback.

Our guns had changed since we first started robbing banks too. At first we carried the cap-and-ball revolvers we were familiar with during the war, but about 1872 the American arms manufacturers finally resolved a patent dispute that allowed the manufacture of cartridge pistols.

The new pistols were better in every way. They ac-cepted readily available cartridges in standard calibers, many of which were interchangeable with the ammuni-tion used by our carbines. My personal arsenal typically consisted of a couple of heavy revolvers, of .44 or .45 cali-ber, a lever-action Winchester, and a double-barreled shotgun. I would also conceal at times a pocket pistol or two, just for emergencies.

The Pinkerton assaults on the James and Younger fami-lies had one result that I'm sure the bearded Scotsman in Chicago would never have anticipated: Both Frank and I married.

The conflict seemed to sharpen our senses, and per-sonally, I had never felt so alive. The long periods of depres-sion that I had suffered during the war and immediately after vanished, and I found myself actually enjoying the little things in life—meals with family and friends, music, the laughter of children.

It's an odd fact of life that when you have nothing left to lose, you don't care about life and will accept just about anything that folks choose to dish out. But when something you love is at risk, you tend to cherish it a little more closely and want to protect it. That's how I felt about my relationship with Zee.

She had stuck by my side during the nine long years of our engagement, ever since she nursed me back to health during the last year of the war. There were times when I had gone weeks or even months without seeing her or so much as writing, and often she feared I was dead. Sometimes, all she knew was what she read in the papers. But she never complained. After Frank and I became celebrities, she told me she considered herself lucky because there were at least a thousand girls who would trade places, no questions asked.

"But why?" I asked her. "Don't you want a normal life?"

"A normal life would not include you, Jesse," she said. "Besides, it's always been interesting. Sometimes, it's been so interesting that I could hardly stand it, but that's the price you pay when your fiancé is Mr. Jesse Woodson James."

The month after the Pinkertons came to Missouri and we sent them home in coffins, Zee and I were married at the home of her sister at Kearney.

The preacher was Zee's uncle, and he argued passionately against the marriage. He tried to reason with her that marriage to an outlaw was bound to end in tragedy, that we never would have any kind of home life, and that the children of such a union would be born in disgrace. When he failed to convince her, he met me on the street outside the house and gave me all the same arguments.

"Did she tell you that she loved me?" I asked.

"Of course," Uncle Billy said. "But—"

"Have I told you that I love her?" I asked.

"You have now," he said. "But love is nothing to base a marriage on, Jesse. There are bigger issues at stake."

"What could possibly be bigger than love?"

"Responsibility, for one thing," the preacher said. "Marriage is the cornerstone of our civilization, and only citizens with clean consciences should enter into it. I mean no disrespect, Jesse, but you take your living from the sweat of other men."

"I steal from the Yankee banks and the railroads," I said. "They've stolen from us for years."

"But they do it legally," he said.

"Do you think God recognizes a difference between stealing with a gun and stealing with a piece of paper? Do you think the carpetbaggers are somehow more honest than I am?"

"Well," he said. "I don't know."

"Look here," I said. "I think it takes a heap more guts to stick a gun in somebody's face and take their money than it does to sit at a desk and order somebody's land to be seized because they can't make your sky-high interest payments."

"But nobody gets killed," he offered.

"People die," I said. "They die of heartbreak, or of shame, or they blow their own brains out because they can't afford to feed their families. People die all the same; it's just that the bankers and the railroads don't have to watch when it happens."

"I'm sorry," he said, "but I can't condone this marriage."

We were alone in front of the house. I was standing beside my horse, and he was clutching his Bible to his chest. I felt like pulling my pistol to convince this hypocrite, but I chose an equally universal, if less violent, solution.

"Look here," I said. "What's the usual fee for hitchin' somebody? Ten bucks?"

"Five dollars is customary," he said.

I reached into my pocket and pulled out a roll of greenbacks.

"How about twenty?" I asked.

"I've made my position clear," he said.

"Forty?"

No reply.

"I'm not going to let you break Zee's heart," I said. "You are her uncle, and she wants you to marry us. Nobody will know about this except you and me. Let's make it a fifty."

"Well . . ."

"What the hell," I said. "Let's go for a hundred. It's a nice round number, and it should buy you enough whiskey to ease your conscience. What do you say to that?"

He took the money and folded it into his Bible.

"Welcome to the family," he said.

Zee and I honeymooned in Texas.

Frank eloped with his sweetheart, Annie Ralston, that June. Her father was a judge in Independence, and Annie was a schoolteacher with a couple of college degrees, so Frank rightly assumed her family would have been less than thrilled to learn they were getting an ex-guerrilla for a son-in-law. They were married at Omaha, Nebraska, and Annie's family did not know her fate until two years later.

Frank and Annie joined us in Texas for a spell, and married life seemed splendid and carefree. But by and by the money began to get scarce, and so we returned to Missouri. We pulled two or three low-risk jobs that we ordinarily would have been ashamed to have our names associated with, just to get by. Then, a couple of weeks before Christmas in 1874, we prepared to rob the Kansas Pacific Railroad.

We had chosen Muncie, a little town just west of Kansas City, because it was out of the way and was close to the Missouri border and all of our usual escape routes. There were five of us, including old hands Cole Younger and Clell Miller. Bob Younger, who reasoned that he was going to be hounded by the Pinkertons no matter what he did, was the newest member of the gang.

Originally, we had planned to rob the train a week before Christmas, but our plans changed when the weather turned bitterly cold and the sky looked like snow. We thought it best if we could pull the robbery while travel was still easy, and let the posse deal with the ice and snow. So we moved the schedule up a week or so, and crossed the line into Kansas on December 8.

We arrived at Muncie in the middle of the afternoon so we would have time to reconnoiter the area. There wasn't much to the place, really, just a spot in the tracks where the railroad had chosen to place a maintenance shack. A telegraph road also crossed the tracks here, and some other buildings had sprung up—there was a restaurant, a blacksmith, and a few widely spaced homes. But it was cold that afternoon, and the businesses had closed up and none of the local residents were inclined to venture outdoors.

We rode up a little hill and waited in the tree line while we surveyed the tracks. Frank had a pair of field glasses, and we passed them around.

The only creatures we spotted was a four-man section crew, and that temporarily caused us some confusion. They would certainly try to interfere with the robbery, unless we posted a couple of men as guards. But that would leave us only three for the robbery, and experience said that was not enough.

"Whoa," Cole said as he looked through the glasses. "It is getting a little crowded down there."

I grabbed the glasses.

Three riders came down the tracks toward the section crew. They had their faces covered against the wind, and they stopped as they met the crew and tried to engage the workers in conversation, but without much luck. It was a still afternoon and we could hear the foreman's voice as he told the riders to "piss off."

All of a sudden two of the riders pulled pistols from their pockets, and a third produced a Winchester from a saddle scabbard. The workers glared at the riders for a moment, then threw down their tools.

"What's this?" I asked.

"It looks like they're going to rob them," Frank said as he took the glasses away from me.

"No, they're not," Clell moaned.

"How do you know?" I asked.

But Clell didn't answer.

As we watched, the riders forced the men to pile ties on the track. Then, when the barricade was finished, they forced them all into the maintenance shack and chained the door shut.

"Dammit," Frank said. "They're going to rob the train."

"You've got to admit they're gutsy," Cole said.

"But it's our train," Frank protested. "What are the odds against it?"

"Pretty damn long," Cole said.

"Say, Clell," I called over. "How did you know they weren't going to rob those section hands?"

"Shit, fellows," Clell said. He had the field glasses now. "That one with the Winchester down there is my little brother, Ed. I guess I shouldn't have said anything to him about our plan."

"And he thought he'd beat us here by a week," I said, "grab the money, and let us take the heat for the job, right?"

"It looks that way," Clell said.

"That's great," Frank said. "Who else have you told about this? The newspapers? Why don't you just wire a message to old Pink himself?"

"Wait," I said. "This may work out for the best. Remember what the *Times* said about us being daring enough to rob those other fellows? Well, let's do it."

"When's the train due?" Cole asked.

"Twenty minutes," Frank said.

"I don't know," Cole said. "We've got three men with guns down there who aren't going to like the idea."

"Those aren't men," I said. "It's Clell's little brother, Ed, and two of his friends. Do you really think they're going to argue with us? Besides, we'll cut them in. Small shares, of course."

"I'm with Jesse," Frank said.

Clell started to speak, but I told him to shut up.

"You created this mess," I told him. "You don't get a say."

"Jesse," Cole said, "this is not the plan we agreed on."

"Well, I'm the leader here, and I say the plan has changed."

Cole shook his head.

"Stay behind if you want," I said as I nudged my horse forward. "But I swear, Cole, you're getting more like an old woman every day."

"To hell with you, Jesse," Cole said as he spurred his horse past me toward the tracks. "One of these days your half-assed plans are going to get us all killed."

Ed Miller was a little more than surprised to see his brother and the rest of the James Gang ride down out of the woods. Ed was just nineteen, too young to have ridden in the war, and he had a small, pinched face and quick, dark eyes.

"What're you doing, Ed?" I asked.

"Hi, Jesse," he said, smiling a rat smile. He was on the ground, beside his horse, looking up at us. "Nothing."

"Well, it looks like you've got designs on our train," Frank said. "Your brother told us you overheard him talking about it. Now, you're planning to rob it and let us take the blame, aren't you?"

"Frank," Ed said. "Jesse. I wouldn't do that. This is just a coincidence."

"Shut up," Clell said. Then he rode over and backhanded his little brother into the middle of next week. The Winchester clattered to the ground.

The section hands began to beat on the door of the shack and demand to know what was going on.

"Jesus," Ed said as he jumped up. He was holding his jaw, and blood was running from the corner of his mouth. "You didn't need to do that, Clell."

"You're lucky I don't kill you," Clell said.

"He's right," Cole said. "We ought to. All three of you."

"Here's how it's going to work," I said. "We're going to rob this train, and you're going to help us. Each of you will get a cut, but not a full cut, because you tried to horn in on our campaign. And you have to follow the other rules of our code as well, which means if you get caught—and you talk—the rest of us will hunt you down and kill you. Not only will we kill you, but we'll skin you just like Captain Anderson did."

"We won't talk," Ed said. "Nothin' could ever make us talk. Right, fellows?"

His friends agreed.

"Who are they?" I asked.

"The ugly one is Buddy McDaniels," Clell said. "The really ugly one is named Billy Ryan."

"What do you think, men?" I asked.

"I think we'd better get ready," Cole said. "Here comes the train."

It was full dark now, and way down the tracks we could see the jittering headlight of the locomotive.

"Set those ties on fire," I said.

We flagged down the train as it approached, so it wouldn't crash and we'd have another wreck on our hands like we did up in Iowa. Then we ordered the train crew to uncouple the baggage and express cars, so the engine wouldn't try to pull away with us inside.

While the others covered us on the ground, Cole and I swung open the door of the express car and pointed our pistols at the messenger.

The messenger was a rather helpful soul, and he opened the safe without protest. He handed over several canvas bags containing bundles of greenbacks, then he paused and looked closely at Cole Younger. "Are you Jesse James?"

"No," Cole said disgustedly.

"And I ain't Cole Younger either," I said.

Not only did we get the payroll that was bound for parts west, we also got several boxes of jewelry that were being shipped to a store in Junction City.

The job went off without a hitch. Nobody was hurt or killed, and we rode away with fifty thousand dollars and change in our saddlebags. It was our biggest casino in a long while.

The railroad, of course, had a fit. They posted a five-thousand-dollar reward for our capture, and the governor of the state of Kansas, Thomas A. Osborn, matched the amount. An additional bounty of one thousand dollars was offered for any of us that could be brought in, dead or alive.

The robbery, of course, was a slap in the face to the Pinkertons. They were supposed to be the best. But if they couldn't protect the railroads from us, what good were they?

A sad note to the story is that Ed Miller's friend, Buddy McDaniels, couldn't handle success. A few days after the job he got roaring drunk in Kansas City on his thousand-dollar portion of the Muncie loot. So drunk, in fact, that a local policeman arrested him for public intoxication—and in Kansas City that is no small trick. When McDaniels was searched before being thrown into jail, the police found some of the jewelry from the holdup in his pockets.

The poor kid was immediately charged with train robbery, but he never confessed and he never betrayed us. Before his trial he managed to escape from the Kansas City jail, and he gave the authorities a pretty good run before he stumbled into the wrong field and was shot dead by a farmer.

18

Greek Fire

FRANK AND I stayed clear of the farm during Christmas 1874, because we reckoned the Pinkertons would be keeping a close watch on the place. We bided our time and spent a pleasant holiday with our wives in the little rented houses we had in Kansas City, then exactly one month later we saddled our horses and rode alone to the family spread in Clay County.

The country was blanketed with snow and we were pleased to see smoke curling from the chimneys and the yellow lights of the home place when we rode up on the evening of January 26. After hiding our horses in the barn, we took our sacks of presents and carried them up onto the porch, where Zerelda swung open the door.

"I was worried about you two," she said.

"Shouldn't have," Frank said.

"Stop talking and get in here," she said. "You never know who's lurking about."

"Nobody followed us," I said.

"Just the same," she said. "There's a new man over at the Askew place, and he's been a little too curious about what goes on here to suit me. Always on our side of the fence, chasing a lost calf or on any other pretext he can think of."

"What's his name?" Frank asked.

"Ladd," Zerelda said.

"We can have a chat with him if you like," I suggested.

"No, stay away from him," Zerelda said as she bolted the door behind us. "He gives me a bad feeling."

"He'd better be careful," Frank said, "or *he'll* be the one with a bad feeling."

We shed our hats and coats, then unbuckled our gun belts and looped them over the back of a wooden chair near the door.

"Look at you two," Zerelda said. "Have you been spending all your money on clothes?"

"Not all our money," Frank said.

We had placed the sacks in the middle of the kitchen, and twelve-year-old Archie couldn't resist poking through them. John Thomas, who was three years older, pulled him back and told him to wait, that we had to eat first.

"Let him pass out the presents," I said.

"For goodness' sake, Jesse," Zerelda said. "You're just as bad as the children. The table is set and the food is ready."

"They've waited an entire month for us," I said. "Don't make them wait any longer. Besides, I see Pappy has started without us."

"He's used to eating at five o'clock," Mother said. "You know how he is, you can't really explain to him that we're waiting on somebody."

I knelt down on the floor and started passing out the gifts: a flute for Archie, a pocket knife for John Thomas, a doll for Fannie.

"She's twelve," Zerelda said. "Don't you think she's a little old for that?"

"You're never too old for dolls," I said.

"I love it," Fannie said, and hugged me.

"Well, then. Did you boys get me a doll as well?" Zerelda asked.

"Let me see," Frank said, and reached into the other sack. "I don't remember if we brought you anything or not. Here's a sweater for Pappy, to keep him warm while he's sitting outside of an evening. Some more toys. Oh, what have we here?"

Frank withdrew a small box. He studied it for a moment, then held it to his ear and shook it.

"Who's this for, Jesse?" he asked me.

"Give me that," Zerelda said, and snatched it away.

Frank laughed.

Zerelda removed the lid. Inside was a teakettle with a wicker handle. She held it up so everyone could see.

"Open it up," I said.

She swung open the lid. Inside was a roll of greenbacks tied with a red ribbon. The bills were of various denominations, and totaled a thousand dollars.

"Boys," she said.

"Don't say a word," Frank warned her. "If we can't afford to share our good fortune with our mother, then money is just no good to us."

"The kettle is your Christmas present," I said. "The rest is for your birthday."

In four days Zerelda would turn fifty.

Still clutching the money in her right hand, Zerelda threw an arm around each of us.

"There's another gift in here for Susan," Frank said, referring to our married twenty-six-year-old sister. "Would you please give it to her when she comes to visit?"

Perry had been busy placing food on the table, but he had watched us out of the corner of his eye the whole time. My mother had started paying Perry and Aunt Charlotte a wage, at least when times were good, but it was barely enough to keep them in the sorry clothes they wore.

I had brought a gift for Perry as well, a harmonica, and as we sat at the table, I gave it to him. He took it and mumbled his thanks without looking me in the eye. Then he said he had to carve the ham.

"That's all you're going to get out of that one," Zerelda said as she took her place at the head of the table. "He's broken more plates since he's turned thirteen than I have in my entire life. The older he gets, the more he takes after his mother."

"Be still," I said.

"Well, it's the truth," Mother said defensively. "Besides, who are you to shush me?"

"I'm twenty-seven years old," I said. "I reckon I'm old enough to have an opinion around here. Or are you the only one who has that right?"

Zerelda looked away.

"You'll have to excuse Jesse," Frank said. "He's a little frayed around the edges because we haven't seen any action in a couple of months. Apologize, Dingus."

"Sorry I spoke roughly, Mother."

"Never mind," Zerelda said. "We're together again as a family, and that's what counts. I wish you could have brought your wives, but I understand the weather is just too bitter."

"It's not that, Mother," Frank said. "If Jesse and I get jumped on the road, we don't want them in the middle of a gunfight."

"Let's join hands and give thanks," Zerelda said. Then she nudged Pappy, who was about to go to sleep, and we held hands while Mother made up a prayer as she went along.

"Thank you, Heavenly Father, for bringing my eldest sons back safely to me," she said. "Your merciful and protective arm has been ever with us, and has sheltered this humble home in the darkest hours this land has known. We are confident that You will bring an end to the oppression that we still endure, that justice will eventually triumph, and that our enemies will know the full weight of Your terrible wrath. May they suffer as we have suffered. In Jesus Christ we pray, Amen."

I woke around midnight.

The north wind had died down and the house was deadly quiet. Frank and I were sleeping on the floor of Mother's bedroom, in front of the fireplace. The rest of the family was asleep throughout the house, and there was hardly a snore coming from any of them.

But something had caused me to rouse, although I did not know whether it was a noise or my own uneasy dreams. I threw the blanket off and sat up.

"Frank?" I asked. "Did you hear something?"

But Frank was fast asleep.

I heard the baying of a hound on a far ridge, and thought that, perhaps, was the cause of my discomfort. I eased back down but could not return to sleep.

Then there was the sound of breaking glass.

I don't think there is a worse sound in the world than a window breaking in the dead of night. Frank and I were up in a moment, and when we threw open the door to the kitchen, we saw the room bathed in fire and a weird phosphorescent glow.

The window facing the porch was broken. In the middle of the floor, among the shards of glass, was a sputtering ball of flame that burned with an unnatural chemical brightness—so bright, in fact, that you could not look directly at it. As it rolled across the floor, it had shed drops of phosphorus, which were eating their way into the planks. The thing had also been wrapped in turpentine-soaked rags, and they had unwound and now lay like a Medusa's head of burning snakes around it.

"My God," Mother screamed behind us.

While Frank and I raced for our pistols, bracing ourselves for the attack we were sure would come, Zerelda grabbed a broom and knocked the thing into the fireplace. It evidently was made of metal, because it clanked when it hit the stones.

"What is that thing?" I asked Frank as we crouched beneath the window. The porch had been soaked with turpentine, and it was on fire too.

"I don't know," he said.

Of course the rest of the family was up now, and little Archie was standing wide-eyed beside his mother as she swatted at the burning spots of fire on the floor.

"Get back in the bedroom," Zerelda said.

Then the thing in the fireplace exploded with a force that slammed Frank and me into the wall and blew the rest of the windows out.

I was unconscious for some minutes. During that time I was again in the dream I had as a child, of the glowing balls of light and floating naked high above the farm. Looking down, I could see our home in flames.

When I came to, Frank was over me.

"Jesse," he said. "I need your help."

Archie was stretched out on the floor, and Zerelda was kneeling over him. Her right arm dangled at a peculiar angle, and as I rushed over I could see that most of her hand and forearm had been blown away by the blast. Archie had an arm that was twisted as well, but there was also a gaping wound in his left side that you could stick your fist into, and blood was flowing out like a river.

"Get some sheets," Frank shouted to Aunt Charlotte and Perry, who were standing in the doorway. Fannie was backed into a corner of the kitchen, crying, and John Thomas was crouching next to her. Perry and Aunt Charlotte were stamping out the remaining spots of fire inside the kitchen.

We frantically bandaged Zerelda's arm and stuffed rags into our little brother's side. As Pappy knelt down to have a look, I grabbed him by the shoulders.

"You're a doctor, remember? Is there anything else we can do?"

Pappy poked gingerly at the wound, then looked up and shook his head.

"Murder," he said.

Zerelda began to sob.

Pappy began chanting.

"Murder, murder," he said. "Murder."

"John Thomas," Frank called. "Come here and take care of them the best you can. Jesse and I have to put out the fire on the porch, or the cabin is going to burn to the ground."

We took up our guns and, in our longjohns, ran out onto the porch. There were figures moving at the edge of the light thrown by the fire, and I emptied my revolver at them. Then Frank pulled me down behind a fence just off the porch as the intruders shot back.

Splinters rained down as bullets chewed into the board just above my head.

"Your bomb has blown our mother's arm away," I shouted as I reloaded from the gun belt looped over my shoulder. Frank, meanwhile, was throwing handfuls of snow up onto the blazing clapboard and into the eaves. "And you have mortally wounded an eight-year-old child. How can you call yourselves men?"

I blazed away again at them, and I could see glimpses of them as they shrank away into the night. Enraged, I dashed into the night after them.

"Cowards!" I screamed. "Why don't you stay and fight if you want us that badly? Or do you prefer to murder women and children?"

"Jesse," Frank called. "The house."

I holstered my gun, found a bucket, and began scooping snow on the flames as well. In a few minutes it was out.

"Do you think they're coming back?" I asked.

"I hope so," Frank said.

Inside, Pappy was still chanting. Zerelda was on the floor, holding Archie in her lap with her left arm. They were both covered in blood. Archie was awake now. He wasn't crying, but he was gazing at her face with trembling eyes.

"Please," he said weakly. "Don't let me die."

Frank pulled John Thomas aside.

"Brother," he said, "you must fetch a doctor, and you must ride like you have never ridden before. Take one of our horses, and don't stop for anything until you've reached help."

"No, Frank," I said. "One of us should go."

"But I can do it," John Thomas said.

"I know," I told him. "But this is our fault. They were hoping to flush us out of the house and then shoot us down. It wouldn't have happened if we hadn't come back."

But at that moment a neighbor named Hall appeared at the kitchen door. He had been summoned by the explosion, which had been heard for miles. He was ordinarily a difficult old fart to get along with, but now he simply shook his head at the human suffering and asked what he could do.

"A doctor," Frank said.

Hall nodded.

"Pinkertons?" he asked.

"Who else?" I spat out.

"My horse is at the rail," he said. "I will be as swift as possible, but it will take at least an hour. It is none of my business, of course, but you boys might think about leaving before folks who are prone to ask a lot of questions start snooping around. As far as I'm concerned, you were never here."

There was nothing the doctor from town could do to save Archie. A fragment of the bomb casing had traveled nearly all the way through his torso. He died just before dawn, still asking his mother to save him.

Zerelda's arm was amputated at the elbow.

Some patches of blood was found in the snow where I had shot at the intruders, and a .32-caliber pistol was discovered. It was engraved with the initials P.G.G.

The new hired man next door, Jack Ladd, had been a Pinkerton operative sent to spy on the farm. When he reported that Frank and I had arrived, a special train was dispatched and stopped on the Hannibal & St. Joseph tracks, three miles away. A squad of detectives then made their way through the snow to the cabin, and what they lobbed through the kitchen window was an explosive shell wrapped in a cloth soaked in Greek fire—a flammable concoction that included phosphorus and turpentine.[1]

The midnight attack outraged the public, and the Pinkertons attempted to deflect responsibility by claiming the device was not a bomb. Instead, they insisted, the device was merely intended to smoke the occupants out. It exploded, they said, because it had been swept into the fireplace.

---

[1]Documents recently discovered show the device was an incendiary bomb manufactured for Pinkerton at the U.S. Rock Island Arsenal. Pinkerton's orders to his operatives were "above everything destroy the house."

So intense was the cry for justice that the Missouri legislature authorized an investigation, which was led by Adjutant General George Caleb Bingham. Now, Bingham had been a Union officer during the war, but he is best remembered for his famous painting that portrays the callous treatment of Missourians under Order No. 11. The picture he painted in words of the Pinkerton assault on the James farm was no less effective.

A Clay County grand jury indicted Allan Pinkerton and several employees of his detective agency with the murder of my little half brother, but he was never brought to trial. There was also some talk in the Missouri legislature of offering Frank and me amnesty, but nothing came of that either.

Sometime after the bombing, I wrote to Pinkerton through the newspapers.

"Oh, Pinkerton," I said. "If you have a heart or a conscience, I know the spirit of my poor little innocent brother hovers around your pillow, and that you never close your eyes but that you see his blood ebb away from the awful wound in his side. You may vindicate yourself with some people, but you cannot fool God. Justice will be done. Some of us boys who fought in the war may have been forced by circumstances to do terrible things, but as God is our witness, we never threw a bomb into a house of sleeping children at midnight."

On April 12, old Dan Askew, our neighbor who had employed the Pinkerton agent, was found shot to death. Some said the Pinkertons silenced him so he couldn't testify against them, but others said it was one of the James boys who sent him to his final reward. But I don't suppose it matters much now who killed him, because he's dead all the same.

And that's what counts.

19

A Daring Plan

THE WOODEN STEPS groaned as Cole Younger ascended them to the big front porch of the Monagaw Springs Hotel. A steward appeared immediately at his elbow.

"Glad to see you again," the young man said. "May I take your coat? Would you care for a refreshment?"

"To hell with refreshments," Cole said as he shrugged off his linen duster. "Bring me a whiskey."

The steward folded the mud-stained duster neatly over his arm, and he pretended not to notice the heavy Colt in its holster and the cartridge belt strapped around the outlaw's waist.

"Right away," the steward said. "Your friends are—"

"I see them," Cole said as he walked across the porch to where Bob Younger and I sat. There was a bottle of laudanum on the table, and as Cole approached, I slipped it into my pocket.

"That stuff is going to kill you," he said.

"My chest has been aching since the Pinkerton attack on the farm," I said. "All that running around in the winter air, I think."

"That was two years ago," Cole said. "But one excuse is as good as another, I reckon."

Bob stood and shook Cole's hand, then they grabbed each other by the shoulder and embraced.

"Damn, it's good to see my little brother again," Cole said as he sat down.

"You've been in my thoughts," Bob said.

The steward brought some shot glasses and a bottle of whiskey and placed them on the table with a flourish. Then he poured two of the shot glasses full, but I held my hand over the third.

"Would you care for another iced tea?" he asked.

"No, thank you," I said.

I slipped a coin into his hand, and he was off.

"Heard you had a kid," Cole said.

"That's right," I said. "Jesse Edwards James."

"Jesus Christ," Cole muttered. "Just what the world needs, another one of you."

"I'll let that remark pass," I said. "Things have been going right well for Zee and me. Frank too. We've been living in Nashville, and acting just like regular businessmen."

"I'm thrilled," Cole said. "What's this cockeyed plan of yours?"

"It's a real corker," Bob said enthusiastically.

"I know you're for it," Cole said. "That's why I'm here. Let Dingus tell it."

"You know Charlie Pitts and Bill Chadwell?"

"Yeah, the ones who were with us when we wrecked that train up in Iowa," Cole said. "They robbed the bank at Baxter Springs in April. Didn't get much, I hear."

"That's the pair," I said. "Well, Chadwell was born in Minnesota, and he tells me that things are just booming up there. They've got so much money, they don't know what to do with it all."

"Minnesota?" Cole snorted. "Isn't that a little far out of our territory?"

"That's the beauty of it," Bob said. "Nobody will expect us to hit a bank up there. It will be just like shooting fish in a barrel."

"What do you mean, us?" Cole asked. "You're not a member of this gang, Bob, and it's going to stay that way. We've already buried one member of this family because of the James-Younger Gang, and that's one too many. Besides, you've got more potential in you than being an outlaw."

"It seems to suit you well enough," Bob said sullenly.

"It's the only thing I know," he said. "If I could do something else, I'd do it."

"That's why I wanted to talk to you," I said. "I know how much you want to go to Cuba, or someplace else in South America, get away from this life and start over."

"Cuba is not in South America," Cole said. "Besides, Jesse, when have you ever been interested in my welfare?"

"We're all in this together," I said. "All for one and one for all, as the saying goes. Besides, I've been thinking those pretty thoughts too, about escaping to some faraway paradise, where we wouldn't have to always be watching over our shoulders for the Pinkertons. Having a kid does that to you."

"I wouldn't know," Cole said.

"One really big job. Then we retire."

Then, a little softer, Cole asked: "Do you have a town in mind?"

"Northfield," I said.

"Jesus the Christ," Cole muttered. "Did you leaf through an atlas and pick this town for the name?"

"That's just an added bonus," I said. "What better place for our last hurrah?"

"Or Waterloo," Cole said.

"No, not Iowa," I said. "Northfield. I'll admit I've never been there, but Chadwell has. He says it is ripe for the taking, and full of squareheads who wouldn't know how to fight if their lives depended upon it. And do you know who deposits their money in this bank at Northfield?"

"Tell him," Bob urged.

"Adelbert Ames and Spoons Butler."

Ames and Butler were a pair of carpetbaggers who had bled Mississippi dry after the war. Ames had been governor before the state legislature impeached him, and Butler was nicknamed Spoons because he was liable to steal the silverware.

"We don't know the country," Cole protested.

"But Chadwell does," I said. "Like the back of his hand."

"It's a stupid plan," Cole said. "I don't like it."

Bob crossed his arms and leaned back in his chair.

"Well, I do," he said. "It's a damned good plan, and I'm throwing in with Jesse even if you don't."

Cole poured himself another shot of whiskey.

"What does Frank say?" he asked me.

"Frank is with us," I said.

"Who else?"

"Clell Miller," I said. "You know Clell."

"And Jim?" Cole asked Bob. "What does your brother Jim say?"

"If I go," Bob said, "he goes."

"I'll be go to hell," Cole said. "Bob, I'm asking you as your brother not to do this. It's a foolish plan. Those squareheads may love their money even more than they love their lives."

"My mind is made up," Bob said defiantly.

Cole threw the whiskey down and wiped his mouth with the back of his hand.

"All right," he said finally. "You have got my arm twisted behind my back. But I'm going only to protect Bob and Jim as best I can. They are my brothers, and I owe them that. When do we go?"

"Just as soon as we get the money together to finance the trip," I said. "It will just take one little job, and then we'll be in business."

"Hell," Cole said. "Broke as usual."

On July 7 we robbed the Missouri Pacific outside Otter-ville, Missouri. We flagged the train down as it slowed to make a curve on one side of the bridge they were con-structing. Cole insisted, however, that Bob not be in-cluded in this robbery in our home state, so we replaced him with a talkative fellow named Hobbs Kerry.

Kerry got himself arrested right after the robbery be-cause he was flashing his money around and bragging about his new career as an outlaw. He spilled his guts too, but by the time authorities knew the James Gang had struck again, we were in Minnesota.

We took the train to Minneapolis, then spent the next week or so in a whorehouse called the Nicollet House while we got our bearings. We bought horses and posed as stock buyers while we visited locations in southern Minnesota, and at one point we changed plans and decided to rob a bank in Mankato. We went so far as to change a fifty-dollar bill there, but there was so much activity on the street that we called things off at the last minute. Then we went back to the origi-nal plan.

On September 7 we rode our horses across the metal bridge leading into Northfield.

"I'll be damned," Cole said. "It's the governor himself."

On the street, walking toward us, was Adelbert Ames. He was with a young boy and an older man. We took them to be his father and his son.

"Governor," Cole said, and tipped his hat to Ames, but extended a middle finger over the brim as he did so.

20

Northfield

"WE'RE GOING TO rob this bank," I said as I placed the barrel of my .45 against the tip of the man's nose. "Don't any of you holler. We've got forty men outside."

Bob Younger and my brother Frank jumped over the counter.

"Well, what's wrong with you?" I asked.

"Eh?"

"Throw up your hands, damn you."

We were the only customers inside the First National Bank of Northfield, Minnesota. There were three employees, including the teller at the counter, who was rubbing noses with my revolver. His name was Bunker, and he was a young man with a high forehead and a broad mustache. He wore a business suit and an expression of disbelief. When I lowered my gun to join my comrades on the other side of the counter, the well-oiled muzzle had left a perfect black ring on the man's nose.

Already, things were going wrong.

Back home, people minded their business. Up here, everybody was interested in what you were doing, either from suspicion or curiosity. The five members of our gang we had left outside had their hands full because every damn fool that passed stopped to ask them where they were from and what they were doing. As we had approached the bank, the owner of the hardware store around the corner followed us and nearly managed to walk right into the bank with us before Clell Miller pulled him back. Miller had been stationed at a hitching post outside the bank, pretending to fool with his saddle, and had already chased five squareheads away. But when he grabbed Miller, he didn't count on him squirming from his grasp and starting to scream bloody murder. Another man, who had been watching the scene from across the street, joined in.

"Get your guns!" We could hear the shouts. "They're robbing the bank! They're robbing the bank!"

We hadn't even gotten a chance yet to play our can-you-change-this-bill-for-us game. Getting the hell out of there would have been the safe thing to do, but then, if I'd always chosen the safe thing, I wouldn't have been a bandit. So I decided that since we were already inside the bank, and probably were going to have to shoot it out anyway, we shouldn't leave empty-handed.

Of the two other employees in the bank, one was sitting at the cashier's desk in front of the vault, and the other was standing in the bookkeeper's area at the back.

"Are you the cashier?" I asked the bearded man at the cashier's desk.

"No, I am not," he said.

"Is he lying?" I asked the other two.

"No, he's not," the teller with the dirty nose said. "That's Mr. Heywood, our bookkeeper. Our cashier is in Philadelphia at the Centennial Exposition."

"Then who the hell are you?" I asked.

"I'm Bunker," the teller said.

"And him?" I nudged my revolver in the direction of the third employee.

"That's Wilcox, the assistant bookkeeper."

Then a rock crashed through the window.

"Jesus H. Christ, Dingus," Frank said. "What's going on out there?"

I went back over the counter and surveyed the street from a window. Two men were throwing rocks at Clell Miller, who was attempting to mount his horse, which was hitched in front of the bank.

"Stop it!" Clell said, and waved his pistol at them.

More rocks.

"Do you want me to kill you? Stop it!"

He fired a round into the air.

Clell put his foot in the stirrup and was about to swing up in the saddle, when another Northfield citizen, armed with a side-by-side shotgun that still had its hardware store tag dangling from the trigger guard, let go with both barrels.

I flinched, but Clell's face had only been peppered with birdshot. His cheeks were bloody, but he wasn't hurt otherwise. If it had been buckshot, as I had assumed, it would have blown his head off.

The birdshot assassin ran away, and the rocks started again. Then I heard a rebel yell and the booming guns of Cole Younger and our other gang members. They attempted to clear the street by shooting into the air.

I jumped back over the counter.

"They're fighting us with birdshot and rocks," I said.

"Crazy sonsabitches," Frank said.

I turned my gun back to Heywood.

"You're lying," I said. "I know you're the cashier. Get off your ass and open that safe damned quick or I'll blow your head clean off."

"I can't," he said.

The vault door was open, so Frank stepped just inside to examine the safe. It was a huge double-doored affair.

"My threat goes for you other two as well," I said. "Open that safe."

"We can't," Bunker pleaded. "None of us know the combination."

"Of all the—" Frank said, getting ready to cuss a blue streak. He was leaning against the doorjamb, just inside in the doorway of the vault, his gun lowered in an off-hand way.

Suddenly Heywood leaped up from his desk, over-turning his chair in the process, and tried to push Frank inside the vault and swing the heavy iron door shut.

Frank was caught between the door and the jamb, and his pistol discharged into the floor. Bob Younger caught Heywood by the collar and pulled him backward, while I waved my pistol at the other two and told them to kiss the floor.

"Buck, you all right?" I asked.

"Sonuvabitch," he said, cradling his left hand. Blood was running down his fingers. "He nearly crushed me, the crazy sonuvabitch. You got a knife? Shooting is too good for him. We ought to slit his throat right here."

I knelt down and pulled a case knife from my pocket, opened it, and held it to Heywood's throat.

"Is this what you want?" I shouted. "To have your neck opened up like a pig?"

"No," Heywood said. "But you'll just have to go ahead and cut my throat. The safe is on a new chronome-ter lock that won't open until the end of the day."

"What kind of lock?" I asked.

"Chronometer," Frank said. "Like a watch. A time lock."

"Shit," I said.

Bunker, the teller, had slid over to the wall and was now inching his way up it, trying to get to his feet.

"Where do you think you're going?" Bob Younger

asked, and kicked him back down. Then he put his pistol against Bunker's temple and cocked the hammer.

"Are you going to tell us where the money is," Bob said, "or am I going to have to splatter your brains all over this nice clean floor?"

Bunker closed his eyes but said nothing.

Bob moved the gun a few inches to the right and fired.

Bunker jumped, and the bullet went through the wall of the vault and ricocheted around inside, scattering tins of jewelry and papers.

Defeated, Bob turned away.

"What is wrong with these squareheads?"

"They're fools, that's what," I said. "You can't reason with them like you can normal folk. Anybody in this situation would help us out, wouldn't they?"

"It's not our money," Heywood said.

"What?" Frank said, and pointed his pistol at him.

"It's not ours to give," Heywood said. "The people around here have worked hard for that money, and they trust us to keep it safe for them. Now, if we helped you, we wouldn't be doing our jobs, eh?"

"I hate the way these jarheads talk," Frank said.

"So you know the combination?" Bob screamed.

"We can't open the safe," Heywood said. "We told you that already. It won't open until four-thirty. You gentlemen can stick around if you like, but it sounds like things are getting a little hot for your companions. It would be good to leave now, eh?"

"Shut up," Frank said.

Outside, the shooting was getting heavier, and I could tell from the heavy boom of the guns that our boys were taking rifle fire and buckshot. I jumped back over the counter and dared a look in the street. What I saw made my heart sink right to the floor.

A regular battle was taking place.

Our boys weren't shooting into the air any longer.

The townspeople had armed themselves with shot-guns and rifles from the hardware store around the corner and made a shooting gallery of the street in front of the bank. Most of the defenders were in good positions. Some were shooting from the second floor of the brick hotel across the street, others were hiding behind the corner of the building, while a few sniped from store-fronts and stairways. Two of our horses were dead at the rail, Clell Miller was on foot trying to get back to the bank, and the others were racing up and down the street trying to find a spot that wasn't exposed to the deadly crossfire.

At that moment a blond-headed Swede darted across the street, apparently in an effort to find safety, but he did not understand the warnings that Cole and the others were shouting. He fell, facedown, in the mud.

Not far away was the body of one of our gang members, Chadwell, who had been shot through the heart. Charlie Pitts was uninjured. Cole Younger was bloody but still mounted, and his brother Jim had taken a round in the shoulder.

"I don't believe this," I muttered.

"How's my brothers?" Bob asked.

"They're still up," I said. "Let's go, Frank. Chadwell is dead. We're through here."

"No," Frank said. "We're not leaving without the money."

He was in a rage now. He swept some papers from the counter, opened the cash drawer, and started scooping out coins and bills. While Frank was throwing his fit, Bunker bolted from the counter area into the director's room in back.

Frank fired but missed, then chased him out into the

street. Just as Bunker made it to the safety of an adjacent building, Frank fired again, and this time the bullet struck him in the right shoulder.

When Frank returned, he calmly reloaded.

"The game is up, boys," he said.

At this instant Cole Younger rode to the front door of the bank. He was bleeding badly from a leg wound, his face and hands were black with powder, and his guns were smoking.

"Get out here, damn you," he called. "They are killing our men."

Bob Younger and I were at the door in a moment, but Frank lingered. He jumped up on the counter, then turned back to look at Heywood, who had gotten up from the floor and was almost to his desk. Frank fired at him but missed, then cocked the revolver again.

"Damn you," he said.

Frank shot him in the forehead.

Heywood's brains dribbled out the back of his head while his body went over backward in the chair.

"Nothing in life," Frank said, "became him so much as leaving it."

21

Heaven Falls

Now, LET ME share a secret with you before I describe the hell that was waiting for us on the street: The safe was unlocked during the entire robbery.

Heywood and the others had told the truth, sort of, about not being able to unlock it. I mean, you can't unlock a safe that is already unlocked, can you? The door was swung shut, and the bolts driven home, but the combination lock—and it was an ordinary, run-of-the-mill combination lock, by the way—had not been spun.

All we would have had to have done was just walk over, turn the handle, and open the damn thing. I'm sure there was a fortune in that safe, or else they wouldn't have sweated so much about it. And there we were, a gang of bank robbers without equal, and we let ourselves be defeated by an open safe.[1] The amount of cash we took totaled $26.70. The only fools at Northfield that day was us.

As I said, our gang was in serious trouble.

---

[1] In 1892 a new generation of outlaws, the Dalton Gang, would fall for this same tactic and be shot to pieces with hardware store guns on the streets of Coffeyville, Kansas.

We nearly stumbled over Clell Miller's body as we left the bank. He had been shot through the torso by a rifle bullet at about the time Cole, who had been shot three times, called to us for help. Jim Younger had taken one round in the shoulder and another in the mouth, and the teeth and bone peeking from his wound made him look like a monster.

Frank mounted his dun. As I mounted my horse, I felt the white-hot sting of a bullet pass through my left calf, and about the same time Frank cried out that he had been struck in the thigh.

Bob Younger discovered that his mount had been shot dead. On foot, Bob blasted away and ran for the cover of some outside stairs. While reloading there, he was hit in the right arm. The ball had shattered the elbow, and his right hand and forearm were useless. He switched his revolver to his left hand and kept shooting. Cole rode over to him, and while Bob was climbing up, somebody missed and shot the saddle horn off. Cole grabbed the horse's mane while Bob held on behind.

Then we raced out of Northfield in the general direction of Missouri. They say from the time we entered the bank to the time the last shot was fired was only seven minutes. It seemed more like seven days to me.

We stopped along the banks of the Cannon River, where we washed and bandaged our wounds using strips torn from our clothing. Our fine clothes had been turned into bloody rags. All of us had been hit, but Frank and I were lucky—no broken bones or punctured vitals. The Youngers had taken the worst of it. And, of course, we were short one horse.

"What now, Frank?" Cole asked as he tucked Bob's arm inside his shirt so it wouldn't flop around. "Chadwell was supposed to guide us out of here. He's dead, and we don't know the country. We need a plan."

"What do you think, Jesse?" Frank asked.

"I don't care what he thinks," Cole said. "I've had enough of his plans. We wouldn't be in this situation if he hadn't talked us into coming up here."

"Shut up, Cole," I said. "We can go at it later, if you want, but right now we don't have time. First, we're going to steal a horse."

As if in answer to our request, a farmer appeared leading a horse that pulled a two-wheeled cart of lumber. When he drew up to us on the riverbank, we pointed our pistols at him and relieved him of the horse. It did not have a saddle, but we stole one at the next farm.

Then it began to rain.

For the next week we slogged through the back country of Minnesota and managed to evade a posse that reached one thousand men, although we never got more than fifty miles from Northfield. Because of our wounded and our unfamiliarity with the country, problems stymied us that we never would have given a second thought in Missouri. We spent days figuring out how to cross rivers and get around lakes, and we were forced to steal chickens for our dinner. Back in Missouri, a hot meal would have been waiting for us at practically any farmhouse, and a sympathetic doctor in every town.

Bob's wound was getting worse, and he had lost so much blood that he was continually confused and unable to stay in the saddle at anything more than a walk. Jim was hardly in better shape, because his shoulder had gone rotten and given him the fever.

We were exhausted and always hungry, but dared not stop for more than a few hours at a time. Add to that the continual wet, and the relentless attack of mosquitoes, and you will have some idea of the hell we endured.

The rivers and towns had wonderful names—the Blue Earth, Elysium, Lake Crystal—but they hid an unpleasant country. I began to hate those names, and had this haunting feeling I was trapped in a gruesome fairy tale.

Finally, on September 14, we had to face the inevitable. Bob and Jim were too weak to go any farther, and we either had to split up and leave the most severely wounded behind, or we all had to make one last stand together. In the shadow of a railway bridge, where we had sought a little protection from the rain, the James-Younger Gang had its last war council.

"What's it going to be?" I asked.

"To hell with you," Cole said bitterly. His hand was on the butt of his gun.

"We've got to make a decision," Frank pressed.

"Bob is played out," I said.

"What do you suggest?" Cole asked. "Do you want to put a bullet through his brain so he won't slow the rest of us down? That's not the way we do things, Jesse."

"That's not what I was proposing," I said. "But we might as well, because it will be more humane than seeing him die slowly out here in the rain."

"Jim ain't much better," Frank said.

"I can't believe you called yourself his friend," Cole told me. "And you, Frank. What the hell has happened to you? Don't the years we spent riding together with Quantrell mean anything to you?"

"You've got no right to speak to me that way," Frank said.

"The hell I don't," Cole spat out. "I've got every right, because I don't know the Frank James who walked into that bank in Northfield. You killed that teller for no good reason, and now you want to leave my brothers to die. Is this what marriage does to you, Frank?"

"Leave Annie out of this."

"You get married and suddenly running back to your wife is more important than standing with your friends?"

Cole asked. "What about you, Jesse? You're married too, and with a family. Are you worried about getting home by supper? Well, it never seems to have bothered you much when you brought Zee the clap from those whores in Tennessee."

I pulled my pistol and Cole pulled his, and in a moment we each had the barrel of our guns to each other's temples. My finger was on the trigger, and not lightly, as I stared into Cole's bloodshot eyes.

"Do it," he said.

"You first."

"I'll not," he said, "but neither will I lower my piece."

Pitts, who had watched all this without saying a word, now unlimbered his piece and pointed it at my head.

"If Cole doesn't mange to kill you," he said, "I will."

Frank grabbed my gun and forced the barrel down.

"Stupid asses," he said. "The posse is going to kill us soon enough. Why do the job for them?"

Pitts lowered his gun. Cole made a disgusted sound in the back of his throat, then jerked his pistol away and returned it to his belt.

"Let's not fight each other," Frank said. "We've been in tough places before."

"Not like this," Cole said. "I'm not afraid of dying. You know that, Frank. But the difference here is that I'm ashamed. Look at what I've let happen to my brothers."

"We're not suggesting killing them," Frank said. "But the posse can take care of them a sight better than we can."

"We ain't surrendering," Bob said weakly. He had been leaning against a timber, and we all thought he was asleep until he spoke.

"The Youngers stick together," Cole said. He walked over, knelt down, and put a hand on his brother's good shoulder. "What do you want to do, Robert?"

"I can't go much farther," he said. His eyes were closed, and his face was turned up. Tears were streaming from the corners of his eyes. "Let Frank and Jesse go. It's not their fault. And I reckon that posse is going to kill us when they catch us, so let's make a stand and die fighting."

"Jim?" Frank asked.

"I'm with Bob," he mumbled through his bandages.

"What about you?" he asked Pitts.

"I reckon I'll stay with these boys," Pitts said. "Captain Younger and I go back to before the war, and I think it's only right that I see this thing through with him. But I wish you good luck, and I'd like you to take this back to my wife."

Pitts slipped a silver chain over his head and handed it to Frank. At the end of the chain dangled a gold nugget.

"It was a charm," he said. "It was supposed to attract what we were after. But I guess the only thing it really attracted was lead."

Then Cole and the others began giving us personal effects—letters, photographs, rings. It was like attending a funeral, only the guests of honor were still breathing.

Finally, they turned away.

"Cole," Frank said.

"Go on," he said. "Get out of here."

"Would you at least shake my hand?" Frank asked.

"Why should I?"

"Because I won't go unless I know we're friends," Frank said. "I'm sorry, Cole. I let you down. It won't happen again."

Cole snorted.

"What kind of a promise is that?" he asked. "I'll be dead in twenty-four hours, and you—well, it'll probably take them a little longer to get you."

"Then what are we arguing about?"

Cole turned around, grasped Frank's hand, and shook

it vigorously. "Farewell, damn you," he said. Then we all shook hands.

We rode off and were soon swallowed by the rain and the darkness.

Frank and I stole horses and survived by petty thievery all the way to Nebraska, where we sold our last pair of horses and boarded a train for Missouri. When I arrived in the middle of the night at the back door of the little house where Zee was waiting in Kansas City at the time, a lamp was burning and she was waiting at the kitchen table.

"Jesse," she said. "Is that you, or your ghost?"

"It's me."

She took a few steps toward me.

"Are you hurt?" she asked. "Do we need a doctor?"

"Shot in the leg," I said, "but a doctor was kind enough to patch it up in South Dakota."

"At the point of a gun, I'll bet," she said as she rushed to my arms and buried her head against my shoulder. "Your brother—he's well?"

"About the same as me," I said.

"Thank God. I've worried about Annie."

Then she held the back of her hand to her nose.

"It is you," she said after a moment. "I reckon a ghost wouldn't smell so. You smell like you've been rolling in horse manure, Jesse."

"Sleeping in it, most of the time," I said. "It is good to be home."

"Home?" she asked. "We've never had one."

"Home is in your arms," I said, and kissed her tenderly.

"My God, Jesse, I thought you were dead," she said. "I'm not going to cry in front of you, because I've got no tears left. You can't do this to me again. I can't live like this."

"You knew what I was when you married me."

"Nobody knew who you were then," she said. "Now the whole damn country is looking for you. It's in every paper."

"They know it was me and Frank?"

"Not for certain," she said. "But it's a good guess, isn't it? The papers have been full of speculation. Cole Younger and the others—"

"Cole's alive?"

"Of course he is," Zee said.

"God damn him. I should have killed the sonuvabitch."

"Hush up, Jesse. You don't know what you're talking about. The Younger boys are going to spend the rest of their lives in prison up north, and you're home with me."

"You almost sound sorry I escaped."

"You know better than that, Jesse," she said. "I'll fetch the papers in a minute so you can read for yourself what your friends said about you. Come on, let's get you out of those filthy clothes and cleaned up."

She lit the stove for some hot water while I placed my guns on the table. My body felt like it had been dragged all the way from Minnesota. Then Zee fetched the newspapers from the other room and placed them in my lap.

Cole and the boys, the papers said, had made it for another week after we split up, until September 21, when the posse cornered them at a place called the Hanska slough. There was a helluva fight. Charlie Pitts was shot dead.

But your typical Younger must be harder to kill than your average cat, and even though the boys went down under a hail of bullets and were shot just about to pieces, they all lived.

Cole had eleven bullets in him. Jim took another round near the spine. When poor Bob stumbled out of their hiding place after his brothers were down, waving a handkerchief in surrender, somebody shot him in the chest.

The Youngers were in wretched shape. They were suffering not only from the bullet wounds, but also from the effects of living like animals in the swamps for nearly two weeks. When they removed Cole's boots after the fight, for example, his toenails came with them.

But after their capture, Minnesota treated the Youngers in a manner better than any state or federal official had ever treated them. They patched them up, fed them, and placed them under heavy guard so the citizens of Northfield couldn't lynch them. The surgeon general of the state even came to examine Jim's terrible mouth wound, and all of them were allowed to have visitors—thousands, in fact, crowded into the jail to catch a glimpse of the famous Missouri outlaws. Cole was talkative enough, and used the opportunity to try to explain how they had been driven to a life of crime by the war. Bob refused to talk about his reasons for becoming an outlaw, and Jim was so ashamed of his ruined face that he sat with his back to them.

Time after time they were asked by reporters and lawmen to identify their accomplices in the Northfield raid. None of them would answer.

"We tried a desperate game and lost," Bob Younger told the papers. "We are rough men and used to rough ways and we will abide by the consequences."

But the burning mystery for the Northfield community was the identity of the robber who had killed Heywood, the cashier. After intense questioning by the local sheriff, Cole said he would sleep on the matter. The next morning he handed the sheriff a written statement.

"Be true to your friends," it said, "if the heavens fall."

22

Revenge

NORTHFIELD PUT AN end to the James Gang, at least for a couple of years.

The body of poor Clell Miller was embalmed and placed on display for a spell as a curiosity in Minnesota, at least until his family managed to obtain a court order to take him home and bury him in Missouri. The corpse of Bill Chadwell was sold to a medical student for dissection, and Charlie Pitts was sold to a doctor in Minnesota, who placed him in an iron cage and sank him in one of those cold lakes. When spring came, the doctor mummified the body and sold it as an exhibit to a carnival sideshow. When it was discovered that few people would pay to see a dead outlaw that didn't bear a famous name, the sideshow began claiming the corpse was that of John Younger.

Frank and I left Missouri and made our homes in Tennessee, where we assumed aliases and tried out best to follow the straight and narrow. While Cole Younger and his brothers were making barrels as convict laborers serving life sentences at the Minnesota State Penitentiary, Frank and I were working for wages at a barrel factory in Nashville. We were Misters Woodson and Howard.

But we never held regular jobs for any length of time.

I caught malaria from the damned mosquitoes in Tennessee and had to borrow money in order to survive. When I couldn't repay the amount, I bought cattle with a fraudulent check and managed to float for a little while longer. But eventually, sickness and bad luck took their toll, and we were forced to move in with Frank.

That's where my daughter, Mary Susan, was born on July 17, 1879. Frank had a child of his own by then, and was enjoying the fruits of a steady life, but I just couldn't seem to make the legitimate life work. So while Frank remained in Tennessee, worked at the lumber company, and took care of both our families, I returned to Missouri and the life I knew best.

My new gang consisted of Ed Miller, one of my cousins, and some lesser known ex-guerrillas. The cream of that crop, of course, was rotting in prison. But I suppose the new boys did well enough when we robbed the Chicago & Alton Railroad at Glendale, Missouri. Nobody was hurt, at least not seriously, and the take was about fifty thousand dollars. I hate to admit it, but things just weren't the same without Cole Younger.

Frank and I were blamed for the robbery, of course, but this time the authorities were only half right. I returned to Tennessee, bought some racehorses, and managed to wrest a few moments of pleasure from the tedium of life by gambling.

The problem with the new gang is that they couldn't keep their mouths shut like the old one had.

Tucker Bassham was arrested for the Glendale job and sentenced to ten years in prison. Soon after that Ed Miller disappeared, and folks began speculating that I did away with him so he wouldn't talk, but that is just rubbish. The truth is that I shot Miller when he pulled a gun on me during an argument about going to the law, and in my book that is self-defense.

Then I robbed a government paymaster at Muscle Shoals, Alabama, and one of the new gang—a drunkard by the name of Bill Ryan—was taken into custody after throwing his money around. Ryan was extradited to Missouri to stand trial for the Glendale robbery, and the bastard Bassham struck a deal with the authorities and agreed to testify against him.

Well, you can see how things were going.

Frank and I left Nashville and set up homes in Kansas City for a spell. Frank reckoned that if he was going to be blamed for jobs he had no hand in, even though he was trying his best to live a normal life, he might as well go back to robbing.

We also needed new gang members to take the place of the ones who had been taken by the law, and our cousin Wood Hite introduced us to twenty-five-year-old Charles Ford.

Charlie was a slight young man from Clay County who had grown up hearing tales of the James boys' exploits, and he said he wanted to be just like us. I was skeptical. His pale skin made it seem he had never spent a day in the sun, he seemed awkward holding a gun, and his eyes seemed never to focus directly on you when he talked. But we were short of men, so Frank and I reluctantly agreed to take him on.

On July 15, 1881, we robbed a Rock Island train near Winston, Missouri. That particular train was chosen because we had learned the conductor, William Westfall, had been in charge of the train that had delivered the Pinkerton men to bomb our house years earlier.

The idea of revenge appealed to Frank. It was one of the few times that we had an opportunity to strike back at someone who was directly involved in the bombing. So, to be sure of our prey, we bought tickets and boarded the train at Cameron, Missouri. The other members of the

gang boarded at Winston, and just outside the station, we
struck.

A couple of boys went forward and ordered the engineer to stop the train. As soon as we ground to a halt,
three others—including Charlie—went back to deal with
the express car.

Frank and I, who were in the smoking car, pulled revolvers from beneath our dusters and leveled them at
Westfall.

"What the hell is this?" he demanded.

"What kind of moron are you?" I asked.

"I reckon you are here to rob us," Westfall said.

"That's part of it," Frank said.

"What do you mean by that?"

"Don't you recognize us, Mr. Westfall?"

"Should I?" he asked.

"My name is Frank James," he said. "And this is my
brother Jesse."

"Oh, Lord," the conductor said.

"Do you remember where you were on the night of
January 26, 1875?" I asked.

Westfall said nothing.

"You were helping a bunch of Pinkertons murder our
little brother," Frank said.

It got really quiet in the smoking car. There were a
dozen passengers, mostly men, and they acted like they
were trying to sink right into the floor.

"That wasn't the plan," Westfall said. "I'm sorry it
happened. The Pinkertons were wrong. Nobody should
have died that night, least of all your little brother."

"Put your damned hands up," Frank said.

"Look, I didn't even leave the train."

"Is your mother living?" I asked.

"I was only the conductor."

"Can you imagine what it is like to see her arm blown

right off, and then to watch as she cradles your little brother on the floor while the life slips out of him?"

Westfall's hands slowly went into the air.

"He begged us not to let him die," Frank said.

"I'm sorry."

"Turn around," I said.

He did so.

"Beg us," Frank said. "Beg us not to kill you."

"No," he said quietly.

"Beg, damn you!" Frank shouted.

"I will not," Westfall said.

Frank placed his revolver against the back of his head and pulled the trigger. In an instant Westfall was sprawled in the aisle, his face in a pool of his own blood.

Frank shot him again, in the back.

One of the male passengers made a furtive move, as if to draw a gun, and I killed him. Then Frank and I shot the living hell out of that car while the other passengers dove for cover.

23

Death Watch

THE MURDER OF Westfall proved to be very unpopular in the press, and even our old friend John Newman Edwards could defend us only by claiming we weren't there.

The governor of Missouri, Thomas Crittenden, offered a reward totaling twenty thousand. When one of my neighbors in Kansas City asked me if I'd like to join a posse that was hunting for the James boys, it was clearly time to find a new home. We moved to another section of Kansas City.

Because Charlie had acquitted himself reasonably well during the Rock Island job, we included him in another train robbery, this one on September 7, 1881, at Blue Cut. Nothing was exceptional about the holdup except the sorry manner in which it was executed; to stop the train, we piled rocks on the track, and a freight nearly plowed into us from behind. Charlie shot at the brakeman who dashed down the tracks to warn the approaching train, and it was a good thing he was a poor shot, or we probably would have all been killed.

Zee and I moved several more times in the coming months, but eventually we moved clean out of Kansas City and settled in a house we liked in St. Joseph. The address was 1318 Lafayette, and under the name Thomas Howard I rented it from a city councilman for fourteen dollars a month.

This was the first house in years where I felt I belonged. It was a white frame affair with a fenced yard, and it was situated at the edge of town, on a high bank overlooking the Missouri River. It was perfect should we have to make a run for it in the middle of the night.

Zee was known as Josie to our neighbors, and we called little Jesse Tim. Before long, Charlie Ford had moved in as well, and he frequently brought his little brother, Bob, around, in hope that I would allow him into the gang as well.

Happiness eluded our family, of course. The constant strain of moving and hiding our true identities had taken a heavy toll on Zee. The killing of the conductor, Westfall, seemed to trouble her a great deal more than it did me. Although she remained fiercely loyal, increasingly she began to talk of "what if."

What if, she asked, I gave up the outlaw life and tried just one more time to live a normal life? If I couldn't do that, then what if I turned myself in and trusted to God to provide a fair trial? Finally, what if I were killed—what would become of her and the children then?

Things quieted down a bit after the Blue Cut robbery, and I started looking around for a way to get out of the business. I read in the paper about 160 acres of bottomland for sale near Franklin, Nebraska. I struck up a correspondence with the owner, a man named Calhoun, and even took Charlie Ford with me on a trip to inspect the property. It looked as if it would make a fine living for Zee and me, but there was one problem—I was out of money again. Another job would be required to start a new life, and soon I began to talk to Bob and Charlie Ford about a bank over in Platte City.

Then something happened that changed all our plans.

On January 3, 1882, our half brother John Thomas Samuel attended a belated New Year's party at the community of Greenville, four miles east of Kearney. I don't know why he felt compelled to attend this event, because it was hosted by Uncle Jimmy Rhodus, a Union veteran and rabid Republican. But our brother—who had insisted on being called Johnny since he turned twenty the Christmas before, and had grown an elaborate beard as a symbol of his manhood—had inherited Zerelda's stubborn trait. There was sure to be fiddle music and pretty young women in attendance, and the combination was too powerful for John Thomas.

There was also, unfortunately, plenty of alcohol available. And to complete the tragic picture, the new "Johnny" had taken to secretly carrying a pistol in his pocket.

Before the night was out, Uncle Jimmy and John Thomas had gotten into a drunken argument on the subject of Frank and Jesse James. The old Yankee, of course, said that we were nothing more than common criminals and had invited every misfortune that had befallen our family. John Thomas argued just as passionately that Frank and I had been forced into a life of crime, and that Allan Pinkerton was the person ultimately responsible for the death of little Archie.

Nobody is quite certain who pulled his pistol first, but John Thomas ended up being shot in the chest with a .36-caliber navy. When the surgeon examined him later that night, he pronounced the wound mortal. The ball had pierced a lung. John Thomas was loaded into the back of a wagon and taken home to die.

Frank and I were summoned to the farm to say farewell to yet another brother. We arrived in the middle of the night and stayed beside his bed until dawn was near. John Thomas, however, was unaware of our presence.

"You two are so much alike," Zerelda told me as I sat next to the bed. "Look at him, Jesse. It must be like looking in a mirror. He so wanted to be like you."

"Well, the pistol ball in his chest is a helluva start," I said.

By and by Frank drifted to sleep in a chair by the fire, and Perry came in and placed a quilt over his knees. He offered to bring me a blanket too, but I declined and said I would stay up with mother for a spell. Perry then brought us coffee from the perpetual pot in the kitchen. But as he was handing my mother her coffee—plenty of cream and sugar, and with a big spoon to stir it with—his hand slipped and a few drops splattered across the back of Zerelda's hand.

"Damn you, Perry," she hissed as she arched her hand like a claw in front of her. "I've only got one good hand left, and I'll thank you to be careful of it. I swear, you're as clumsy as *ever* your mother was."

Perry dabbed at Zerelda's hand with a dish towel he kept thrown over his shoulder. His head was down, but the firelight glinting from his eyes told me he wasn't sorry—and reflected for a moment in his fine and sensitive features, I saw Hannah.

"Perry," I said. "Your mother wasn't clumsy."

"She broke a lot of dishes."

"That's because she hated you," I said.

"Of course she did," Zerelda sniffed, "because my poor half-witted husband couldn't keep his hands off her. That's the only reason we kept Perry, you know, because he has Dr. Samuel's blood in his veins."

"Mother," I said, "Pappy's blood has nothing to do with it."

Zerelda stared at me for a moment with wild eyes,

then softly asked Perry to leave us. He looked at me, and I nodded. When the door to the bedroom closed, Zerelda reached across and snagged my cuff.

"It ain't true," she said. "You were too young."

"Decidedly I wasn't."

"I don't believe a word of it."

"The truth always burns a little going down."

"How could you!"

"How could *you*?" I asked. "How could you send her away? How could you separate mother and child? How could you do it to me? Don't you have an ounce of feeling in you?"

"Jesse," she said. "You can't be serious. These people—they aren't like us. They aren't fully *human*."

"You can't think that," I said. "Don't you remember Old Ambrose? Don't you remember how kind Aunt Charlotte—"

"They're like little children," Zerelda went on. "They're not responsible for themselves, they need somebody to look after them. That's what the war was all about."

"Damn you, mother," I said. "That's not why I fought. And if you think it is, I'm ashamed."

As we prepared to leave before first light, and avoid the prying eyes of the detectives who were sure to be near, Zerelda pulled us aside. Her grief was heartbreaking. She hugged each of us and, through her tears, said that she could no longer stand to lose any of her children.

"My sons," she sobbed, "are being taken from me one by one. It is just a matter of time before death claims both of you as well."

"Don't talk like that," Frank said.

"It's true," she said. "The wheel of fortune has

turned. For eighteen years you and Jesse have eluded the Yankees and the Pinkertons, but things have changed so. Too many innocents have died. The age of the gun must pass."

"Mother," I pleaded.

"No," she said. "You both must promise me that you will do whatever is necessary so that you both may live—even if that means turning yourselves in."

Frank shook his head.

"Promise," Zerelda said. "Even if it means never seeing either of you again. Go to the ends of the earth if you must. As long as I know that you are alive and well."

"But—" I began.

"No," she said, and put a finger to my lips. "Don't allow your brother's death to be in vain. Do you not see how Christlike he suffers? Let this tragedy be the last in our family, and signal a new life for you both."

As the weeks wore on, John Thomas remained in a pitiful state—not dead, but not really alive either. His body was ravaged by fever. Consciousness came and went. The chest wound healed over, but the ball remained. The doctors advised us to pray much and to expect little. Every week the newspapers reported that John Thomas Samuel had surely taken his penultimate breath.

Zerelda made funeral arrangements.

Then, early in February, the fever passed and he gained some strength. He was able again to eat some solid food, and to sit up and talk and even joke a little. Surely, we thought, recovery was near. Then pneumonia struck. By the end of the month he had lapsed into a coma, and it was apparent to all that John Thomas Samuel must finally lose the battle.

•   •   •

Before dawn on the first of April, Frank and I were sitting in the dark near the bed, listening to the ragged breathing of our half brother. Zerelda had collapsed from exhaustion and was asleep in the kitchen.

We were alone in the room.

"Frank," I ventured. "I've been thinking."

"Not another job, Jesse."

"What do you think would happen if one of us died? Would things go easier on the other? I mean, you know how the courts and the legislature are swayed by public opinion."

"I'm not drawing straws to see who commits suicide, if that's what you're getting at."

"No," I said. "What I mean is, what if the world thought that one of us was dead. And not just dead, but *assassinated*. In a way that would make people think of the Robin Hood story."

"You mean betrayed by one of his own."

"That's it," I said.

"Well," he said, "it would give us a shot at being heroes again. But folks see you as Robin Hood. I'm just one of the Merry Men. But as much as I hate you sometimes, I'm not willing to let you sacrifice yourself for me."

"I'm not too warm to that idea myself. But I've been talking this over with Bob and Charlie Ford—"

"Not those two!"

"Hear me out," I said. "The police commissioner in Kansas City put them in touch with Governor Crittenden, and he offered them ten thousand dollars if they would assassinate me. Can you believe it? They asked me what they should do, and I said to string them along. Just to see how things would work out."

"I might shoot you myself for ten thousand dollars," Frank joked. "But I still don't see where this is going."

"They have put the authorities off for weeks," I said. "They always tell them that I'm too wary, that they can't catch me without my guns, or they can't get me alone."

"So?"

"What if we let them do it," I suggested.

"That's a great plan, Dingus, except you're still dead."

I paused.

"We've seen a lot of gruesome things, haven't we?" I asked. "We've been shot up and drenched in the blood of our friends. We've seen our little brother blown up and our mother horribly maimed. What if there was something we could do that would be a little unpleasant at the time but would turn everything around?"

"What the hell are you talking about?"

"All these years, and nobody but the family is sure of what either of us looks like," I said. "We could make the death of John Thomas count for something."

24

Up from Thunder

THE SHOCK OF what the stranger had just related transported me jarringly out of those faraway outlaw days and into the present, to the porch of the Bixby Hotel at Hannibal. We had passed the entire night there, fortified by strong coffee and stronger tobacco, and with blankets wrapped around our knees to fend off the chill of the long night. Now the first fingers of dawn were shooting over the Mississippi to the east.

"You don't mean to say that you swapped the body of that poor dead half brother for your own," I said.

"That's exactly what we did," the stranger said with a wicked smile. "Death mercifully claimed John Thomas a few hours before dawn on that third day of April in 1882. Immediately afterward, a gruesome package was smuggled away from the family farm in the back of a wagon."

"Go on," I urged.

"Upon arrival at the little white house at the edge of town in St. Joseph, it was a simple but grisly matter to dress the body in my clothes, place my guns nearby, and prop it up in a chair beneath a sampler that read *God Bless Our Home*. It was a nice touch, I thought, because Zerelda had given us the sampler as a wedding present.

"Then, a little after breakfast time, Charlie Ford

drew his .44 Smith & Wesson, fired a bullet at the back of
the corpse's head, and missed as usual, leaving a hole in
the plaster of the wall beyond. Bob Ford then pulled forth
his .45 Colt and completed the task. They ran out of the
house shouting that they had killed Jesse James. History
handled the rest."

Then the stranger closed his eyes.

"Before the day was out, the *St. Joseph Daily Gazette*
trumpeted: 'Up from Thunder! Jesse James, the Missouri
outlaw, before whom the deeds of Fra Diavolo, Dick
Turpin, and Schinderhannes dwindled into insignificance, was instantly killed by a boy twenty years old,
named Robert Ford.' Within hours the yard of the little
house on the hill was choked with hundreds of people.
The fence was trampled down, the most ordinary household objects were stolen as souvenirs, and folks began
sticking their fingers into the bullet hole in the wall beneath the sampler. Soon the landlord was charging ten
cents admission."

"What happened to the Ford brothers?" I asked.

"After wiring Governor Crittenden that the deed was
done, they surrendered to the St. Joseph police. Two
weeks later they were indicted for murder by a local
grand jury; they both pled guilty and both were sentenced
to hang. They were pardoned by the governor that afternoon. They later claimed they never did see any of the reward money, and I believe them.

"Two years later, Charlie Ford was so depressed over
the hatred heaped upon him for his part in the alleged assassination plot that he walked into a field, placed a pistol
to his head, and blew his brains out. At that distance he
couldn't miss. His brother Bob lasted a little longer, but
in 1892 a man came into his saloon in Colorado and cut
him in two with a shotgun. They say his killer was a great
admirer of mine."

"But what about Zerelda?" I cried.

The stranger sighed.

"Zerelda arrived by train the morning after the announcement that I had been shot. She was immediately ushered into Sidenfaden Funeral Parlor to view the body as it lay on ice. 'This is my son,' she said. 'Would to God that it were not.' The body was later released to her, and it was taken to Kearney aboard a special St. Joseph & Hannibal Railroad train. Hundreds of people filed past the open casket as it was on display in the lobby of a local hotel, then it was taken to the Mt. Gilead Baptist Church, where mourners sang my favorite hymn, 'Amazing Grace.' At the conclusion of the funeral, the crowd was told to avoid visiting the family farm, because half brother John Thomas Samuel lay near death. The shock might push the poor lad into a grave of his own, they warned.

"The casket was buried next to a rail fence in the southwest corner of the yard, beneath the infamous coffee bean tree. Within a year Zerelda was charging the curious twenty-five cents to visit the last resting place of her most famous son, and another two bits if they wished to carry a pebble away from atop the grave. She still lives at the farm with Perry Samuel, who cooks her food and manages the more mundane matters at the historic site. Periodically, Zerelda replenishes the stock of pebbles on the grave from those in the creek behind the house."

The stranger paused.

"My brother Frank, accompanied by John Newman Edwards, surrendered to Governor Crittenden later that year. Frank took out his old guerrilla revolver and offered it butt-first to Crittenden and delivered a little speech he had practiced: 'Governor, I want to hand over to you that which no living man except myself has been permitted to touch since 1861, and to say that I am your prisoner.'

Frank was tried but acquitted of all charges brought against him.

"In 1889 Cole Younger gave a prison interview to the *Cincinnati Enquirer* in which he claimed that all other participants in the Northfield robbery were dead. Later that year Bob Younger, still suffering from his crippled right arm, died of consumption.

"Then last year, in 1901, Minnesota passed a new law that states prisoners who had served at least twenty-five years of a life sentence were eligible for parole, and Cole and Jim Younger were released. Cole took a job as a traveling tombstone salesman, and I hear Jim is selling cigars in Minneapolis."

"Ah," I said. "But you've forgotten something. What about Zee? You haven't told me what happened to Zee and the children."

"Zee," the stranger said, and smiled. "Rather than having to live with her namesake, Zee returned to Kansas City. Thomas Crittenden, the son of the former governor, eventually lent her enough money to build a home there. But she never was the same after April 3, 1882, and her health steadily deteriorated until she lapsed into a coma and eventually died on November 13, 1900. She was fifty-five. The cause of death was listed as sciatic rheumatism and nervous prostration, but it was apparent to all that she had simply died of a broken heart.

"Mary, our daughter, then lived on the James farm with grandmother Zerelda until last year, when she married a neighbor by the name of Henry Barr. Our son, Jesse Edwards James, owns a cigar store in Kansas City, wrote a book last year called *Jesse James, My Father*, and is thinking about going to law school. How's that for irony?"

We fell silent as I digested the information that had just been related. I felt as if I had been under some kind of spell that the stranger had woven with his words, and I wasn't quite sure but that it had all been a dream.

"I know what you're thinking," he said. "You believe I'm a lunatic. Well, I would be the last to claim that I was completely sane, but I have told you the truth. There were a few whoppers thrown in here and there just for flavor, but mainly it was the truth."

"Look here," I protested. "You have not convinced me. Zee is the weak link in your story. I cannot imagine that good woman participating in such an underhanded trick."

The stranger smiled.

"I'll tell you something," he said. "It was really her idea."

With that the stranger rose from his chair and stretched.

"I must be going," he said.

"One last question," I said. "What did you do after?"

"Oh, they say John Thomas Samuel made a complete and miraculous recovery from his wounds a week or so after the burial of his outlaw brother and immediately set out for California. But that, my friend, is another tale."

Editor's Note

ALLAN PINKERTON DIED on July 1, 1884. Three weeks earlier, he had tripped on a Chicago sidewalk and bit his tongue. The wound became gangrenous, septicemia followed, and Pinkerton's death was reported as one of particular agony.

Briefly, the fates of the James Gang who survived after the stranger's story ends:

Jim Younger committed suicide on October 19, 1902, after a failed romance with newspaper reporter Alix Mueller and after going for twenty-five years without a bite of solid food.

Also in 1902, Cole Younger began touring with his old friend Frank James in a wild west show. Frank died on February 8, 1915, of heart failure, at age seventy-two.

In 1913, on the fiftieth anniversary of the Lawrence massacre, Cole was "saved" at a tent revival at Lawrence, Kansas, and renounced his outlaw life. He died on March 19, 1916, at the age of seventy-two. On his deathbed he revealed to Jesse Edwards James that the killer of cashier Heywood in Northfield had been his uncle, Frank James.

Zerelda James Samuel, the mother of America's most famous outlaw brothers, suffered a stroke on February 10,

1911, while returning to the Clay County farm after having visited Frank and his wife, Annie, at their Oklahoma farm. She died on board a St. Louis & San Francisco passenger train, and was employing a "lifetime pass" that had been given to her by railway officials. She was eighty-six.

Afterword

IT SHOULD HARDLY be necessary to remind readers of the number of impostors claiming to be Jesse James who have cropped up since that fateful Monday morning in 1882 when the "dirty little coward shot Mr. Howard."

Serious students of outlaw lore will know that none of them ever presented a convincing argument for being the supposedly dead bandit, but it is left to the field of human psychology to explain just why so many people—including those who ought to know better—were taken in by the audacious lies.

The first notable was John James, who claimed in the 1930s that the man killed in St. Joseph was a stand-in by the name of Charlie Bigelow. He claimed that Bigelow was a rival bandit who had impersonated Jesse during several robberies in the Midwest, and that killing him and substituting his body for Jesse's was a neat bit of poetic justice.

After convincing some of the more gullible residents of Clay County that he was the genuine article, he started lecturing as "Jesse James Alive!" Then he was snapped up by a grandstanding preacher named Robert E. Highley, who used James as a living attraction for his fire-and-brimstone sermons.

Although this J. James was old, and he was a killer, he was certainly no Jesse.

In his middle eighties when he revealed himself as the famous outlaw, John James was on parole from the state of Illinois for killing a man over a fifty-cent debt back in 1926, when he was just seventy-nine. He had apparently concocted the Jesse scheme while reading books about the outlaw during his brief prison term at Menard, Illinois. After his release he traveled to Clay County and started pumping the locals for information that he would use to persuade others he was the real thing.

The James family, however, remained unconvinced.

In a dramatic twist on the Cinderella story, Annie, the wife of Frank James, attended an Excelsior Springs lecture and challenged John James to try on a pair of boots that had belonged to the real Jesse. The impostor, of course, could not jam his feet into the size 7 1/2 boots.

Sadly, many old-timers were quick to sign affidavits for John James, which confused the issue for years. What is left of the legacy of John James is a sad photograph from his days as an exhibit: a gaunt and spectacularly aged man, jammed into a black suit, wearing black gloves, boots, and a laughable black hat, and with a pair of revolvers sitting butt-forward in their black holsters. The expression on his face is that of a little boy playing robber.

John James died in a state mental hospital in Arkansas on Christmas Eve, 1947. Taking this as a cue, perhaps, to trod the stage of pseudohistory was J. Frank Dalton.

In 1948 Dalton was presented to a newspaper in Lawton, Oklahoma, as being the 101-year-old outlaw, and he quickly became the most famous of the posers.

The newspaper bought the story, which led to headlines across the country, which led to Dalton being installed as a permanent attraction by the promoter of Meramec Caverns near Stanton, Missouri.

A story was concocted to link the historical outlaw with the tourist attraction, and a big birthday party for "Jesse's" 103rd birthday was held at the cave, creating even more media attention. Imagine the shock many historians must have received when they learned that among the guests was 106-year-old Cole Younger, who was found hiding in Tennessee. Visitors to the tourist attraction are told to this day that Jesse James and his gang used the place as a hideout.

J. Frank Dalton's leading front man was Orvus Lee Howk, who had brought Dalton to the attention of that Oklahoma newspaper in 1948, and who apparently had coached him using the same "switched at death" story that John James had invented. To bolster his story, Howk even claimed to be Dalton's grandson—and, of course, that his real name was Jesse James III.

Not much is known about J. Frank Dalton other than he sometimes wrote articles about the Old West for East Texas newspapers while working in the oil fields there during the 1930s. He seemed to know so much about the border war—and was about the right age—that many historians thought he may have been a guerrilla himself, but not Jesse James. In 1938 he did apply for a pension as a Confederate veteran, and he listed his date of birth as 1848 in Galiad, Texas. The pension was denied, however, because no federal or state records could be found to support the claim.

The man known as J. Frank Dalton died in Granbury, Texas, in 1951. But even after his death his promoters continued to cash in on the hoax.

Rudy Turilli, promoter of the Meramec Cavern birthday party, published a book in1966 called *The Truth About Jesse James*. It could hardly have had a worse title. Not only did it perpetuate the J. Frank Dalton story, it also offered a $10,000 reward to anyone who could prove that Dalton wasn't the famous outlaw. The grandchildren of Jesse James, among other family, took Turilli up on his offer, and in 1970 they won their case in circuit court at Franklin County, Missouri.

Turilli appealed, lost again, and died in 1972 without paying the judgment.

Meanwhile, Orvus Howk had been busy perpetuating the hoax by erecting a monument on Dalton's grave that reads in part: "Jesse Woodson James," with the explanation, "supposedly killed in 1882."

Howk embroidered the story by claiming that before his death, Dalton—who was really his grandfather, Jesse, remember?—had told him of the many treasures that had been hidden across the Southwest by the Knights of the Golden Circle. The treasures, Howk said, were meant to rearm the South and to fight the Civil War all over again. Of course, he had a few maps available if anybody was interested in seeking these treasures for themselves. Howk died in the 1980s, and the last treasure hunt to employ any of these maps was reportedly directed by his sons in 1992.

William H. Parmley of Locust Grove, Oklahoma, was another would-be Jesse. Parmley died in 1906, but his family believed there was enough evidence left in an old Bible to suspect the two men had switched identities and that the real Jesse James was buried in his grave.

Another posthumous impostor was Jacob Gerlt, who died in 1951. But a grandson became convinced that Gerlt and his wife were actually Jesse and Zee James after a relative brought him a box of photos, gold coins, and other items that fired his imagination. The grandson, Vincel Simmons, published his theory in 1994 in yet another book with an incongruous title, *Jesse James: The Real Story.*

Frank James, too, had his impostors. No less than three old men claimed to be the celebrated Shakespeare-

quoting guerrilla, but their claims were even more out-
landish than those who sought the identity of his infamous
little brother.

The body of Jesse James was moved from the James
farm to Mount Olivet Cemetery at Kearney in 1902 in an
effort to keep souvenir hunters at bay. During the move,
some of the remains escaped from the decaying coffin
and remained at the original gravesite. This material—
consisting of hair, bone, and teeth—was collected in
1978 by the curator of the James farm, and became the
basis for the first scientific attempt to determine if Jesse
James had really been buried there in 1882.

The collected material was mailed in a cigar box to
Michael Finnegan, a forensic anthropologist at Kansas
State University in Manhattan, Kansas. Although Finnegan could not provide a positive identification using these
limited remains (not all of the bones were human, in fact;
some were animal bones that had infiltrated the grave),
he concluded in a professional paper that they were at
least compatible with the historical record of Jesse James.
For example, the bones were determined to be a century
old, and from an individual who was approximately thirty-
eight at the time of his death (Jesse was thirty-four). Also,
the presence of a dental hypoplasia suggested that the individual had suffered a high fever in early childhood, and
Jesse was known to have been seriously ill at age six from
an abscess on the right thigh. Additionally, though perhaps irrelevantly, the hair samples revealed that the individual was infected with head lice.

A .38-caliber bullet from a Smith & Wesson revolver
was also found during the James farm excavation, although experts could not determine whether it was the
fatal bullet.

The remains recovered in 1978 have become known
as the "Tupperware remains" because they were placed

in a plastic container and reburied at the James farm. The finding that the material was merely consistent with the historical record, however, did little to satisfy the curiosity of those who believed there was a chance Jesse had somehow escaped death on April 3, 1882.

The debate simmered until 1995, when advances in forensic science took the James saga in a new direction.

James E. Starrs, a professor at George Washington University, headed an expert forensics team that aimed to settle the question, once and for all, of who was buried in Jesse's grave.

Advances in DNA testing had made it possible to trace ancestry using skeletal remains. Although the DNA testing would be the centerpiece of the team's investigation, other forensics disciplines would be employed as well to gain as much information as possible.

Starrs is a professor of both law and forensics and has published a quarterly newsletter, *Scientific Sleuthing Review,* since the 1970s, and has investigated a number of other famous cases from history. To date, they include the James case, the Lindbergh kidnapping, the Sacco and Vanzetti robbery-murders, the Alfred Packer cannibalism cases, the assassination of Senator Huey Long, the hatchet murders of the Bordens, the CIA-LSD– related death of Frank Olson, and the mysterious death of Meriwether Lewis.

After obtaining the permission of surviving James family descendants, Starrs petitioned the Clay County circuit court for an order of exhumation. The order was granted, but with the stipulation that the remains be reburied within ninety days of the exhumation.

A three-day dig at the gravesite in July 1995—with security provided by the Pinkerton Detective Agency— proved to be more difficult than the investigators had anticipated. The casket was deeper than expected, and not much of it was left. It harbored only a few skull fragments, a tooth with a gold filling, a few arm and leg bones, and a .36-caliber ball found in the chest area.

Enough was found, however, for forensic analysis to begin.

As scientists across the country labored over unlocking the secrets yielded by the 113-year-old grave, preparations were made for the October reburial. It was first suggested that a memorial service be held at the church in Kearney where Jesse had been a member, but the church refused to host the event; plans were then made to hold the funeral at William Jewell College at Liberty, but college officials withdrew their offer when it was learned that a Confederate flag would be prominently displayed.

On October 28, 1995, a service was finally held for Jesse at a local funeral home, and his new poplar coffin was draped with the Confederate battle flag. Afterward, the remains were reinterred at Mount Olivet Cemetery, under the intense scrutiny of the national and international media.

After months of delays, the results of the investigation were finally announced by Starrs in June 1996 at the National Academy of Forensic Sciences convention in Nashville: The team had concluded with a "high degree of certainty" that the remains were indeed those of Jesse Woodson James. Although there was plenty of circumstantial evidence to indicate that Jesse had really been found (the deceased was male, stood about five feet nine inches tall, between thirty and forty years of age, the bullet in the chest area was from an 1851 navy Colt, and there was evidence of a fatal bullet wound to the back of the skull), the real clincher was the DNA evidence.

The DNA extracted from one of the teeth recovered from the Kearney gravesite matched the genetic markers taken from the blood of Robert Jackson, an Oklahoma City lawyer and great-great-grandson of Jesse's sister, Susan.

The question was settled.

Jesse James really was assassinated by that dirty little coward on April 3, 1882, in St. Joseph.

What, then, are we to make of the curious manuscript that was found by historian Gene DeGruson in the Fort Scott, Kansas, junk shop? Certainly it is a hoax, perpetuated by Twain's biographer, Albert Bigelow Paine, or someone else with just enough knowledge of history to make themselves dangerous.

And yet . . .

There is one last thing.

The type of genetic material that is used to trace ancestry in skeletal remains is mitochondrial DNA, which is passed down through female family members only. That means that the investigator's most conclusive piece of evidence was that the body in the grave at Mount Olivet Cemetery was that of a child born to Zerelda James Samuel. And of her male children, there are only four possibilities: Frank and Jesse, of course, little Archie, or John Thomas.

About the Author

MAX MCCOY is an award-winning investigative reporter, freelance journalist, and award-winning author of four previous novels, including, *The Sixth Rider, Sons of Fire, The Wild Rider,* and *Home to Texas.* He is also the author of Bantam's Indiana Jones adventure series.